Erotic Zombies
In The UK

Erotic Zombies In The UK

BY

TRACY WILSON

http://beautifulpublications.com

Published by
Beautiful Publications LLC
Stratford, CT 06614

This book is a work of fiction. Names, characters, places, and incidents are either products of the author's imagination or are used fictitiously. Any resemblance to actual events or locales or persons, living or dead, is entirely coincidental.

Library of Congress Control Number:
2022920521
Print ISBN: 979-8-9855290-7-4
Ebook ISBN: 979-8-9855-290-6-7

Printed in the United States of America

"I miss you so much Kate..." John cried...

"John..."

"I must be tired... I need some sleep..." he said as he climbed into bed...

"John..."

"There it is again..." he said as he got up and went into the kitchen...

"John..."

"Okay – now I know I heard something..." he said as he opened the French doors and went out into the backyard...

"John... Over here..." John went over to the bushes near the fence in his backyard...

"Kate? Am I dreaming?" Kate was on her knees behind the bushes...

"No John... You're not dreaming..." she breathed as she put her hand in John's pajamas and pulled out his dick...

"Kate... Wh... Ooohhh..." he moaned as Kate took his dick in her mouth... "Kate... Kate... Kate..." John moaned as he held Kates head with both hands and pushed his dick in her mouth...

"Mmm..." Kate moaned on his dick and it sent John into frenzy...

"UUGGHH!! UUGGHH!! UUGGHH!! UUGGHH!! UUUGGGHHH!!"

"I love you John..."

"I love you too Kate..."

"I have to go..."

"No... Please... Don't leave..."

"I'll be back... I promise..." she said and then John cried as he saw his wife go back down in the pile of dirt behind the bushes...

"I must be crazy..." he cried as he went back inside... "I'm going to bed..." he said as he went into the bedroom, climbed into bed, and went to sleep...

"Good evening everyone..." Claire greeted...

"Good evening..." they all said...

"Did everyone enjoy our last author?"

"Yes..."

"Uh huh..."

"I did..."

"I guess I did..." John sighed...

""You didn't enjoy the evening John?" Claire asked...

"I enjoyed the evening... but all I could think about was my wife..."

"You're still grieving... that's understandable..." Donna said...

"I was devastated when my wife died – if it weren't for Tales on Tuesdays – I don't know where I'd be right now..."

"I'm glad you reached out to us when you did..." Claire said...

"So am I..."

"Does anyone have any questions or should I end the meeting?"

"I have a question..." John said...

"Yes John?"

"Is it possible to see a loved one after they die?"

"Absolutely..." Donna said...

"Oh thank God – I thought I was crazy..."

"I saw my grandmother in my dreams for about a week..." Donna said...

"I saw a good friend of mine – at least I think I did..." Claire said...

"You think you did?" John asked...

"I realized it wasn't her when I went up to her, turned her around, and it was somebody else..."

"Wow..." Donna exclaimed...

"I need to go... it's getting late here..." someone else said...

"Me too... goodnight..." Claire waited until it was just the three of them before she continued...

"John?"

"Yes Claire?"

"Are you okay?"

"I'm not sure..."

"You're going to see your wife for a while..." Donna said...

"I hope so..." John sighed...

"John – what do you mean?" Claire asked...

"Promise you'll keep this between us..."

"Okay..."

"Promise me!"

"Okay John! I promise!"

"Donna?"

"I promise too!"

"Okay..." John sighed and then he continued... "Last night... I saw my wife..."

"So you dreamed of her..." Claire said...

"No... I saw her..."

"John... it wasn't Kate..."

"Yes it was! I know what I saw – I know what I felt!"

"You know what you felt?" Donna asked...

"Kate came to see me last night..."

"Okay John - where did she come see you?"

"She came to see me at home..."

"John – are you sure you weren't dreaming?" Donna asked...

4

"I was wide awake – I was tired – but I was wide awake..."

"Okay John – you were awake – what happened?" Claire asked...

"I kept hearing my wife call me so I went out into the backyard..."

"Are you sure it was your wife calling you?" Donna asked...

"It was my wife!" John snapped...

"Okay, okay – I'm sorry..."

"I went in the backyard – I looked behind the bushes... and my wife was there..."

"Your wife was in the backyard?"

"Yes..."

"What did she do once you saw her?" Claire asked...

"We made love..."

"WHAT?!" they both exclaimed...

"We made love..." John repeated...

"You made love to your dead wife? In the backyard?" Claire asked...

"Yes..."

"John... that isn't possible..." Donna said...

"You think I'm crazy – I shouldn't've told you..." John sighed as he logged off...

"Claire! What are we gonna do?!" Donna exclaimed...

"I'll reach out to him tomorrow..." Claire sighed...

"John..."

"Kate..." John breathed as he jumped up out of bed and hurried to the backyard...

"John..."

"I'm here Kate..." he breathed as he hurried over to the bushes...

"John..." she sighed...

"Kate..." he breathed as he pulled her up into his arms... "Are you real?"

"How do I feel?" she whispered...

"You feel so good... please don't leave me..."

"I want to stay John... but I can't..."

"No... I won't let you leave me..." he pleaded as he held her tighter...

"I can stay for a while – but I need to go back..."

"Back? Back where?"

"Sutton Hoo..."

"How did you get here?"

"It took me so long to find you..."

"I don't understand..."

"I couldn't rest without you... I needed to come to you..."

"I need you..."

"I heard you crying... I followed your cries..."

"Oh my God... Kate..."

"Let's go inside..." John took his wife by the hand and walked her into the kitchen...

"Can I get you something to drink?"

"John – I don't get hungry or thirsty..."

"I don't understand..."

"Normally when you die, you get buried, you go in the ground, and you stay in the ground..."

"We buried you..."

"Yes... but that was before the soil got fertilized..."

"Before the soil got fertilized?"

"John... do you remember when the government invested in the weed killer to eliminate the Erotic Zombies?"

"Yes..."

"I was buried in Sutton Hoo..."

"I know..."

"Sutton Hoo is a Royal Sacred Burial Ground..."

"I know that too..."

"So... sacred burial grounds can't be disturbed..."

"So... Sutton Hoo never got treated?"

"None of the sacred burial grounds were treated..."

"Kate... Are you telling me..."

"Yes..."

"So... You're an Erotic Zombie?"

"Yes..."

"So... You're alive?"

"I'm dead..." Kate answered as she got up from the table and went over to John... "And I'm horny..."

"Kate... this can't be right..."

"It felt right last night... didn't it?"

"Last night was wonderful..."

"It can be wonderful again..."

"How?"

"Make love to me John... Please..." she breathed as she pulled him into a kiss. John couldn't resist if he wanted to... and he didn't want to. He continued to kiss her and run his hands up and down her body as he held her... "John... Take me to bed..." John took Kate by the hand and led her into the bedroom. Kate let her dirty clothes fall to the floor and she stood there naked in front of him... "John... Take me..." John stripped out of his clothes, went over to his wife, picked her up in his arms, carried her to the bed, laid her down, and got on top of her... "Yes John... Make love to me..."

"Kate... You feel so good..." John moaned as he kissed her...

"Yes John... Yes..." John kissed his wife on her neck and shoulders, and then he moved to her breasts...

"John... Oh John..." John took turns, alternating between kissing, licking, and sucking her breasts... "Yes John... Yess..." she moaned as he kissed his way down her body... "John... Don't stop... Please... I need you... I crave you..." John went between her legs, spread her lips, and dove in... "JOOHHNN!!" she moaned as he licked, slurped, and sucked. John drank his wife's nectar as she began squirting all over his face... "Oh God... John... It's been so long..."

"Yes... it has..." John growled as he got up, moved up between her legs, and thrust himself inside her...

"Kate... Ugghh... Kate..."

"John... Yes..."

"You feel so good Kate... Uugghh..."

"John... harder... please..."

"Kate... Uggh... Uggh..."

"John... I'm cumming... Don't stop... I'm cumming..."

"KATE!!   KATE!!   KATE!! UUUGGGHHH!!" John collapsed on top of her and held her...

"Oh John... I needed you..."

"I don't understand..." he breathed as he kissed her...

"I've been awake and horny ever since you buried me..."

"You've been awake and horny ever since I buried you?"

"Yes..."

"I'm so confused..."

"The erotic zombies are all fucking each other..."

"They are?"

"Yes... and I've been miserable..."

"Kate... I'm sorry..."

"You were my one and only love...I didn't want anybody else..."

"Oh Kate..."

"I know I should've moved on – I should've let you grieve – I should've let you get over me... but the closer I got to you... the more I craved you..."

"Kate... I love you... I missed you... my heart ached..."

'I can't stay here... but I can come back..."

"You promise?"

"Yes John – I promise..." she breathed as she kissed him and then she got up...

"Please stay Kate... please..."

"I'll see you tomorrow..." she said as she put her clothes on. John watched her leave the bedroom and he cried...

"Hello Kate..."

"Who are you?"

"My name is Trevor..."

'Hello Trevor..." she greeted nervously...

"I know what you're craving..." he breathed as he pulled her close to him and held her...

"No... Please... I don't want you..." she cried...

"Kate... I'm not going to hurt you..."

"Okay..."

"As I said..." he whispered and then he whispered in her ear... "I know what you crave..."

"Please don't hurt me..." she pleaded as she started to cry...

"What if I told you I could help you be with John in eternity?"

10

"Can you do that?"

"Yes..."

"Please – tell me what to do – I'll do anything..."

"That's what I wanted to hear..." he breathed as he ran his hands up her body and squeezed her breast...

"Please... don't..."

"I know what you're craving... and I'm craving someone too..." he breathed as he slid his hand in her pants...

"Please... No..."

"I know you want this..."

"Please... I want John..."

"And I want Bazil..." he said as he took his hand out her pants...

"Bazil? Where is he? I'll find him for you..."

"I already know where he is..."

"Do you need me to help you get to him?"

"I need you to help him come to meee..." he breathed as he kissed her...

"I... I can do that..."

"Here's what I need you to do..." he breathed in her ear as he put his hand back in her pants and squeezed her ass...

"Tell me... I'll do it... Just don't hurt me..."

"The next time you go see John... tell him you know a way that you can be together in eternity forever..."

"Okkkay..." she stuttered as Trevor moved his hand under her blouse and squeezed her breast again...

"Tell John I'm going to visit him..." he breathed as he kissed her...

"Okkkay..." she stuttered again...

"Do this for me..." he breathed in her ear as he continued massaging her breast... "And I'll let you continue getting what you crave..."

"You won't hurt me?"

"Do as I said..." he breathed as he kissed her again... "Tell John I'm coming to see him..."

"Okkkay..."

"One more thing..." he breathed as he moved his hands up her back and held her against him...

"Yyesss?"

"Don't tell anyone you saw me..."

"I won't..."

"Promise meee..."

"I won't... I promise..." Trevor kissed her again, let go of her... and disappeared...

"Kate – is that you?" John breathed as he hurried into the backyard...

"Yes John..." John hurried over to the bushes, pulled her up out the dirt, and began kissing her all over her face...

"John... Wait..."

"No..." he breathed as he continued kissing her...

"John..."

"I need to make love to you... now..." John breathed as he pulled her to the ground and pulled her down on top of him...

"John... Wait..."

"Don't make me stop Kate... Please... I need you..." he breathed as he pushed her on her back and slid her pants down...

"John... Yes... Take me..." she breathed as she pushed his pajamas down off his ass...

"Yes John... Take her... Give her what she craves..." Trevor breathed as he took his dick out and began stroking it..."

"Kate... Oh Kate..." John moaned as he thrust himself inside her...
"John... Yes... John..."
"Kate... You feel so good... I can't get enough of you... Uggh..."
"Oh John... Yes... Don't stop John... Don't stop..."
"I'M CUMMING KATE... I'M CUMMING..."
"JOHN... JOHN... JOHN..."
"UUUGGGHHH!!"
"AAAGGGHHH!"

"I'm cumming too..." Trevor gritted as he came so hard his sperm shot across the lawn. John and Kate were so into each other they didn't notice Trevor in the yard with them...

"KEEP IT DOWN OVER THERE!! PEOPLE ARE TRYING TO SLEEP!!" somebody yelled...
"C'mon..." John laughed as he got up and helped Kate up...

14

"I can't believe we just did that..." Kate laughed...

"I don't know what's gotten into me..." John said as they went into the kitchen and sat down...

"We need to talk John..."

"Kate... No... Please don't tell me you can't see me again..."

"John...Listen to me..."

"Okay..."

"Last night... after I left..."

"Oh no..."

"I'm okay... he didn't hurt me..."

"Who?"

"Trevor..."

"Who's Trevor?"

"Trevor's another erotic zombie..."

"Kate..."

"He didn't hurt me..."

"Did he touch you?"

"Yes..."

"Does he know you've been to see me?"

"Yes..."

"What does he want?"

"He wants to help us be together in eternity..."

"He didn't need to touch you to tell you that..."

"John... Please... Listen..."

"Okay..."

"He said he knows what I crave..."

"Oh my God..."

"I told him I want you..."

"I know you want me..."

"He said he craves Bazil..."

"Oh my God..."

"What's wrong?"

"I know who Bazil is..."

"Who is he?"

"Bazil Osgood from Osgood Publishing..."

"Isn't that the man that was on the news for the erotic zombies in Connecticut?"

"Yes..."

"Trevor told me he'll help us be together in eternity if I help him get what he craves..."

"You mean who he craves..." John sighed...

"Trevor's coming to see you..."

"I want to see him..."

"John... Please... Don't make him angry..."

"I won't make him angry – I don't want him to hurt you..."

"I have to go now..."

"Will you be back?"

"Yes John – I'll be back..." John got up, pulled his wife up out the chair, and held her...

"I love you so much..."

"I love you too..."

"I can't be without you..."

"I can't be without you either..."

"I'll help Trevor..." he breathed as he kissed her...

"I'll be back tomorrow..."

"See you tomorrow..."

"No John... You'll see MEEE tomorrow..." Trevor growled...

"Kate..." John breathed as he hurried out into the backyard...

"Kate won't be joining us..." Trevor said as he stepped out from behind the bushes...

"You must be Trevor..." John sighed...

"I am..."

"What do you want?!"

"Please... I can explain..."

"Come with me..." John said as Trevor came into the house behind him... "Have a seat..." Trevor sat down at the table... "Talk..."

"I miss him so much..." Trevor cried...

"Who?"

"Bazil..."

"You? And Bazil?"

"We met in prison..."

"Prison?" For What?"

"That doesn't matter..."

"You're right – I'm sorry..."

"One night... I was in my cell..."

"Oh my God – what happened?"

"He said I had to pay..."

"Bazil was going to rape you?"

"Bazil saved my life..."

'Oh wow..."

"Bazil asked them to transfer me to his cell so he could protect me... and we fell in love..."

"Oh wow..."

"When we got out of prison, we planned to spend the rest of our lives together..."

"What changed?"

"I was killed!" Trevor exclaimed as he broke down in tears...

"Oh my God... I'm so sorry..." John sighed as he pulled Trevor into a hug and held him. Trevor smiled to himself as he cried on John's shoulder...

"Why didn't you go to him like my wife cane to me?"

"I can't..."

"Why?"

"They treated all the areas – we can't live there – I had no choice but to come here..."

"What made you reach out to my wife?"

"I saw your wife leave and come back..."

"You've been following my wife?!"

"No – I only followed your wife tonight – I swear..."

19

"Why were you touching my wife?"

"I would never hurt her – I saw she was miserable without you – and then last night I saw how happy she was – and I knew..."

"About me?"

"Yes..."

"How?"

"She was the only one..."

"The only one?"

"All the other erotic zombies are with each other – your wife was miserable – I'm miserable – I just want to be happy like you and your wife – please – I'm begging you..." he cried... and John fell for it...

"I'll help you..."

"You will?" Trevor asked as he wiped his eyes...

"Yes..."

"Oh thank you! Thank you so much!"

"My wife said you'll help us..."

"I will – but I need your help first..."

"Okay – tell me what you need..."

"I need you to contact Bazil..."

"You want me to tell him I saw you?"

"No! You can't!"

"Why not?"

"He won't believe you! He'll think you're crazy!"

"Okay – what should I do?"

"Tell him about your wife..."

"Tell him about my wife?"

"Yes. Tell him your wife's been visiting you..."

"Why?"

"Tell him you need his help to get your wife back to the afterlife..."

"But I don't want her to go back without me..."

"I know that. You can tell Bazil the truth when he gets here..."

"I can tell him about you?"

"No – I want to surprise him the way your wife surprised you..."

"So what do I tell him?"

"When he gets here – meet with him in person – and then you can tell him the truth is you want him to help you get to the afterlife so you can be with your wife..."

"Wait a minute – I have to die?"

"That the only way you can be together for eternity..."

"I'm not sure I want to do that..."

"Fine – I'll tell Kate you don't want to spend eternity with her then..." Trevor sighed as he got up...

"Wait!"

"Yes?"

"I'll do it..."

"Are you sure?"

"I'm sure..."

"You know this means you have to die – right?"

"Yes..."

"And you're sure you want to do this?"

"I haven't stopped grieving since she died..."

"I know how that feels..."

"And now that she's come back to me – I don't want to live without her..." Trevor smiled to himself...

"You're smiling..."

"Yes..."

"You're thinking about Bazil..."

"Yes..."

"What if Bazil moved on?"

"I won't know for sure until I see him..."

"I hope you get to spend eternity with the love of your life..."

"So do I..." Trevor said as he got up... "Oh – John?"

"Yes?"

"You can't ever tell Bazil you saw me – or spoke to me – even after he gets here..."

"What if he doesn't come?"

"He'll come..." Trevor said as he went out into the backyard... and then he was gone...

"Good morning!" Beautiee sang as she walked in...

"Good morning Mrs. Osgood..."

"Good morning..."

"Good morning..." the employees greeted as Beautiee walked past them...

"Good morning..." I greeted...

"Good morning Mr. Osgood..."

"Good morning..."

"Good morning..." the employees greeted as I walked past them and followed Beautiee into the office. Beautiee looked at me as I locked the door...

"Mr. Osgood – I haven't had my coffee yet..." she said as she walked towards me...

"So what?" I breathed as I pulled her into a kiss...

"So... Joselyn... Will... Interrupt... Us..." she breathed...

"Okay... I'll let you get your coffee..." I breathed just as Joselyn knocked on the door..."

"Mrs. Osgood?"

"Yes Joselyn?"

"I have your coffee..." I unlocked the door and opened it...

"Good morning Joselyn..."

"Good morning Mr. Osgood..."

"I'll take that..." I said as I took the coffee from her...

"Joselyn?" Beautiee called out...

"Yes Mrs. Osgood?"

"I need to see you and Sheila in the conference room at 10..."

"Okay – I'll let my mother know..." she said as she turned to leave and I closed the door behind her...

"Hey..." Sam said when he saw Joselyn...

"Hey..."

"What's wrong?"

"Beautiee said she needs to see me and my mother in the conference room at 10..."

"What's wrong with that?"

"I hope it's nothing serious..."

"Joselyn – the last time we all had to meet in the conference room was because we were all invited to renew our vows with them..."

"Oh yea – you right..."

"Is Bazil here?"

"He is..."

"I'ma go see him right quick..."

"Sam – wait until after 10..."

"Why?"

"Because when he took Beautiee's coffee from me, he locked the door..." she laughed....

"Now..." I breathed as I put Beautiee's coffee on her desk and then I pulled her into my arms... "Where were we?"

"Bazil – I need coffee..."

"Okay – here..." I said as I picked up the cup and put it to her mouth...

"Bazil... I..."

"Drink..." I commanded...

"Yes My Thirst Quencher..." she breathed as she took a gulp. I pulled the cup away from her, put it down, and pulled her into a kiss...

"Mmm..." I moaned as I pushed my tongue in her mouth...

"Bazil... I...."

"Drink..." I commanded as I put the cup to her mouth again and she took another gulp. I put the cup down on the table, pulled Beautiee into a kiss, and pushed my tongue in her mouth again... "Mmm..." I moaned. Beautiee waited for me to put the cup to her mouth for the 3rd time and this time I didn't have to tell her to drink – she took the cup out of my hand, gulped it down, put the empty cup on the desk, and pushed me back towards the couch... "Beautiee..." I panted before she pushed me down and lay down on top of me... "Mmmph..."

"Mmm..."

"Mmmph..."

"Mmm..."

"Beautiee..."

"Yes..."

"Let me make love to you..."

"No..."

"Why?"

"We... have... a... meeting... at... 10..."

"We... have... time..."

"Bazil... stop... I can't..."

"But you want to..." I breathed as I slipped my hand in her pants...

"Bazil... No..."

"You're wet..." I breathed as I rubbed her clit and pulled her to my mouth... "Mmmph..."

"Mmm..."

"Mmmph..."

"Mmm..."

"Mmmph..."

"MMMMM!!" I held Beautiee down as her body shook on top of me... "MY THIRST QUENCHER..." she whispered...

"Yes... I am..." I breathed as I helped Beautiee up, sat up next to her, and licked my fingers...

"Now..." I breathed as I pulled her close to me... "What's this meeting about?"

"I want to know how Shadajah and A'Licia are doing..."

"I'm sure they're doing fine..."

"I'm thinking about giving them a raise..."

"How long have they been working here?"

"About two years..."

"Okay..."

"Mrs. Osgood?"

"Yes Sheila?"

"I'll be in the conference room..."

"Okay – see you in a few minutes..."

"It's only 9:30!" I laughed...

"You know how Sheila is – she probably brought a folder in there – she figures she can get some work done before our meeting..."

"Let's see how much we can get done before 10..." I said...

"Yes..." Beautiee said as she put her hand in my pants...

"Beautiee..." I moaned...

"Yes My Thirst Quencher?" Beautiee looked up at me and began stroking my dick...

"Fuck!!"

"Be quiet!" she whispered. I knew there was only one way I was going to be quiet so I grabbed her, kissed her hard, and covered her mouth with mine so no one would hear me...

"Mmmph..."

"Mmm..."

"Mmmph..."

"Mmm..."

"MMMPPPHHH!! Beautiee... Wait... It's sensitive..."

"So..."

"Beautiee... I can't..."

"Okay..." she breathed as she got up and got down between my legs...

"Beautiee... Ooohhh..." I watched as she sucked me clean and then she got up off her knees, sat back down beside me, and licked her fingers... "Damn..." I breathed...

"It's 9:45 – let's go..."

"Okay..." I breathed as I got up and followed her into the conference room...

"Good morning..." Beautiee greeted as she sat down...

"Good morning..." they both greeted in unison...

"Good morning... I greeted...

"Good morning..." they both greeted in unison again...

"I wanted to meet with you both to find out how Shadajah and A'Licia are doing..."

"Shadajah is doing wonderfully..." Joselyn sighed...

"How about A'Licia?"

"Well – I'll tell ya..." Sheila sighed... "I'm so used to doing everything myself – I didn't give her that much to do – but let me tell you – I gave her some more stuff to do – and I don't know how I was able to get everything done without her!"

"That's all I needed to hear – Bazil – could you go get Shadajah and A'Licia?"

"Sure – I'll be right back..."

"Hey Bazil – I need to speak to you..." Sam said...

"I'll come to your office when we're done – I need to get Shadajah and A'Licia and bring them to the conference room..."

"Okay..."

"Good morning..." Shadajah greeted as she sat down...

"Good morning..." A'Licia greeted as she sat down...

"Good morning – I'll get right to the point..." Beautiee said... "I spoke to Sheila and Joselyn and they let me know they're very happy with you both..."

"Oh thank God!" Shadajah sighed...

"A'Licia – Sheila told me she doesn't know how she was able to get the job done before without you..."

"Mrs. Henley..." A'Licia sniffed. I handed her the box of tissues... "That's the nicest thing anyone's ever said about me... thank you..."

"Oh no – thank you!" Sheila exclaimed...

"I need you both to go see Cheryl in payroll – you need to sign the paperwork so she can process your raise..."

"We're getting a raise?!" Shadajah exclaimed...

"Yes..."

"Oh my God!! Thank you!!" she exclaimed as she threw her arms around Beautiee's neck...

"Shadajah – you're choking me..." Beautiee laughed...

"Sorry – I'm so excited – c'mon A'Licia!"

"A'Licia – are you okay?" Beautiee asked...

"I worked at the hospital for five years – I worked overtime – I did extra work – and all they ever gave me was more work..." she sniffed...

"You're welcome..." Beautiee said...

"Sheila?"

"Yes Mrs. Osgood?"

"I need you to go down to see Cheryl in payroll too..."

"Why – they don't need me to sign anything – besides – I need to finish the report I was working on..."

"Sheila?" Beautiee interrupted...

"Yes?"

"You don't need to sign their paperwork – you need to sign your paperwork..."

"I'm getting a raise too?"

"Yes..."

"Well then – I'll get right on that – and thank you!" she exclaimed as she got up and hurried behind Shadajah and A'Licia...

"I'll see you back in the office Beautiee – I need to speak with Sam..." I said as I got up to leave...

"Okay..."

"Do you need me for anything else Mrs. Osgood?" Joselyn asked...

"No Joselyn – thank you..."

"Okay – I'll see you later..."

"Hey Sam..." I greeted as I walked in...

"You might want to sit down for this..." Sam suggested...

"What's going on?" I asked as I sat down...

"Joselyn went through the mail..."

"Okay..."

"You got a letter from this book club..."

"They want to buy books from us?"

"No..." Sam answered as he handed me the letter and I began reading...

"Dear Mr. Osgood,

My name is John Kirkham. I'm one of the Administrators and Moderators of the Facebook Group, Tales on Tuesdays.

I'm writing to you because I need your help.

My wife Kate died a little over a year ago. When she died, I was devastated and I was

31

depressed. Meeting the members from the Tales on Tuesdays Book Club was the best thing that ever happened to me. I made some new friends and I had something to look forward to. I was finally starting to feel like myself again until last week.

My wife came to visit me. I was able to touch her so I know I wasn't dreaming. I told my friends in the book club and sadly, they don't believe me.

My wife has been to visit me more than once and each time she visits me, she tells me how miserable she is without me. I want to help her get back to the afterlife so she can rest and I can get back to feeling like myself again but I have no idea how to help her.

I saw your story and I saw how you helped your parents so I'm hoping you can help me too. Please don't say no. I don't have anyone else to turn to.

Sincerely,

John Kirkham"

"I need a drink..." I said as I got up...
"Are you okay Bazil?"

"I have no idea..." I sighed as I left Sam's office and went straight to see Beautiee...

CHAPTER 5

"Hey Mr. Osgood..." Beautiee said as she got up from her desk and came over to me...

"We need to talk..." I sighed...

"Come sit down..." she said as she led me over to the couch and we sat down...

"We need to go home..."

"Bazil – what's wrong?"

"I need a drink – and I haven't eaten yet..."

"Why don't we go down to the cafeteria?"

"Beautiee... please... I just wanna go home..."

'Okay – we can leave..." she said as she got up and went to pick up the phone...

"Yes Mrs. Osgood?"

"Could you let everyone know we're gone for the day?"

"Gone for the day? You just got here!" she laughed...

"And now we're leaving..."

"Oookkkaaayyy..." Joselyn said as she hung up...

"Hey Joselyn..." Sam said as she came inside...

"Did you talk to Bazil?"

"Yea – why?"

"Beautiee just called me to let me know they're leaving for the day..."

"Oh boy..."

"What happened?"

"Close the door..." Joselyn closed the door and went to sit down...

"Sam – what happened?"

"I don't know if I should be telling you this – so keep it between us – okay?"

"Okay..."

"You remember that letter you gave me from the Tales on Tuesdays Book Club?"

"Yes..."

"They don't want books..."

"They want an interview?"

"No..."

"Sam?"

"The letter is from John Kirkham..."

"I saw that..."

"He wants Bazil to help him get his wife back to the afterlife..."

"Sam?"

"Yes Joselyn..."

"Are you telling me what I think you're telling me?"

"Yes..."

"Oh my God..."

"Beautiee – I said I wanted to go home..."

"I heard you..." she said as she continued driving...

"Where are we going?"

"You said you needed a drink but you haven't eaten yet – so I'm going to feed you..." she answered as we pulled into Cracker Barrel...

"Why are you smiling?"

"I'm remembering what you did to me in the parking lot..." she sighed...

"I'm sorry..."

"I know..."

"Let's hurry up and go inside..."

"Okay..." she sighed as we both got out...

"Come'ere..." I breathed as I pulled her into a kiss...

"Mr. Osgood..." she breathed...

"Yes Mrs. Osgood?"

"You keep kissing me like that and we're not gonna make it into the restaurant..."

"Mmm... I like the sound of that..."

"So do I – but I need to know what's going on – and you need to eat..."

"Okay..." I laughed as we went inside...

"I'll drive..." I said when we got to the parking lot...

"Okay..." We got in the car and I drove without speaking. Thank God Beautiee didn't push me to talk...

"Hey y'all..." Keisha greeted...

"Hey Keisha..." I greeted...

"Hey..." Beautiee greeted...

"Y'all good?"

"Yea — we're working from home today..." Beautiee answered...

"Aaight — I'll call you later..." she said as went inside...

"C'mon..." Beautiee said as she went to open the door...

"Come'ere..." I breathed as I pulled her into a kiss...

"Bazil... No..." she said as she pushed me away from her...

"Okay — we'll talk..." I sighed as we went into the library and sat down... "Here..." I sighed as I handed her the letter. Beautiee took the letter out the envelope and began reading...

"Dear Mr. Osgood,

My name is John Kirkham. I'm one of the Administrators and Moderators of the Facebook Group, Tales on Tuesdays.

I'm writing to you because I need your help.

My wife Kate died a little over a year ago. When she died, I was devastated and I was depressed. Meeting the members from the Tales on Tuesdays Book Club was the best thing that ever happened to me. I made some new friends and I had something to look forward to. I was finally starting to feel like myself again until last week.

My wife came to visit me. I was able to touch her so I know I wasn't dreaming. I told my friends in the book club and sadly, they don't believe me.

My wife has been to visit me more than once and each time she visits me, she tells me how miserable she is without me. I want to help her get back to the afterlife so she can rest and I can get back to feeling like myself again but I have no idea how to help her.

I saw your story and I saw how you helped your parents so I'm hoping you can help me too. Please don't say no. I don't have anyone else to turn to.

Sincerely,

John Kirkham"

"Oh my God..." she whispered...
"I don't know what to do!"
"Do you want to go?"
"I thought we were done with this..." I sighed...
"I thought so too..."
"I remember how crazy everything was when I saw my parents in the backyard..."
"Oh my God!" Beautiee laughed... "You asked me why I was letting our son watch you argue with zombies!"
"Yes!"
"I'm glad we got to tell their story..."
"I love you so much..."
"I love you more..."
"What if this is just a prank?"
"A prank?"
"What if I go out to the UK and the news & media bombard me with questions and interviews?"
"Do you think they would do that?"
"Have you forgotten News12?"
"That was different..."
"How is it different?"
"Zombies were fucking all over Fairfield and Westchester counties..."
"They could be fucking all over the UK too..."

"We haven't seen it on the news..."

"Doesn't mean it's not happening...

"What if he's telling the truth?"

"Oh God – I hope not..."

"I know – but what if he is?"

"What are you asking me Beautiee?"

"What if you could help him the say way you helped your parents?"

"I'm not sure I want to..."

"I understand..."

"I help him – he tells his friend – next thing you know –his friend is asking me for help – and so on and so on – I don't want that job!"

"Bazil..." Beautiee sighed as she took my hands... "It's okay..."

"You don't think I should go?"

"It's not up to me..."

"What if it were up to you? What would you do?"

"Honestly?"

"Yes..."

"I'd go..."

"Why?"

"I just keep thinking about what would've happened if I never got to meet your parents..."

"You're right – but that has nothing to do with him..."

"I know – but what if it were you?"

"Me?"

"What if something happened to me and I kept coming back to you?"

"Oh that wouldn't be a problem..."

"Why not?"

"Cause you'll never leave me – and if something happened to you – I'd go with you..."

"You're crazy!" Beautiee laughed...

"I'm serious!"

"I know – that's why I said you're crazy!" she laughed...

"Would you really go?"

"I think I would..."

"Why though?"

"Before I started writing books I would've said hell no – but now that I'm publishing books with you, I don't think you should pass up the opportunity to go to the UK – you could come back and end up writing a best-seller..."

"Hmmm – I never thought of that..."

"Does that mean you'll go?"

"I'll go..."

"I wish I could go with you..." she sighed...

"Why can't you?"

"The kids have school..."

"We can have Chandler & Starr watch the kids..."

"I don't wanna do that to the kids again..."

"Do what?"

"Scare them..."

"They were pretty scared..."

"They were also sad because they couldn't come home..."

"True..."

"And there'd be a lot of questions..."

"True..."

"And you wouldn't be able to concentrate..."

"I miss you already..."

"Let's go upstairs..." she said as she stood up and extended her hand to take mine...

"Why are we going upstairs when we can stay here?"

"Because the loveseat isn't big enough..." she answered as she smiled at me mischievously...

"Come'ere" I growled as I pulled her into a kiss...

"Yes My Thirst Quencher..." she breathed...

"Come with me..." I commanded as I pulled her towards the bed...

"I'm coming..." she laughed...

"Not yet... but you will be..." I breathed as I pushed her down on the bed...

"Ooohh!" she exclaimed as I snatched her pants off along with her panties...

"Now..." I breathed as I spread her legs... "Earlier today you sucked my dick... so..." I breathed as I positioned myself... "I'm about to return the favor...

"BAZILLL!! HUH... HUH... HUH... DON'T STOP... I'M CUMMING... HUH... HUH... I'M CUMMING!!"

"Now I'm going to give you what I wanted to give you earlier..." I breathed as I got up, got on top of her, and thrust myself inside her...

"BAZILLL... HA... HA... HA... HA..."

"UUGH... UUGH... UUGH... UUGH..."

"HA... HA... HA... HA..."

"UUGH... UUGH... UUGH... UUGH..."

"I'M CUMMING!!"

"CUM FOR ME!!'

"AAAGGGHHH!!"

"UUUGGGHHH!!"

"That... was... so... fucking... good..." she breathed...

"Yes... it was..."

"I'm glad we came home..."

"So am I..." I yawned as we fell asleep...

"Working hard eh?" Keisha laughed as she finished her coffee...

"Beautiee? Bazil?" Y'all here?"

"I'll get it..." I said as I got up and put my pants back on as Beautiee's cell phone rang...

"Hello?" Beautiee answered...

"Y'all decent?"

"Yea..." she laughed... Bazil was on his way down to answer the door...

"I'll just take the kids to my house..."

"Thank you Keisha..." she said as she hung up...

"Keisha's taking the kids next door?"

"Yea..."

"Good — let's go downstairs in case she changes her mind..." I laughed as Beautiee got up.   Beautiee got dressed and we went downstairs to the office...

"Bazil – look..." I went over to Beautiee's desk and looked at her laptop...

"This flight leaves tomorrow..."

"I know..."

"You wouldn't be trying to get rid of me – would you?"

"Never..."

"Just checking..."

"I was just thinking – the sooner you leave – the sooner you can come home...

"You miss me already?"

"Yes..."

"Okay – book it..."

"You wanna find out if this is a scam?"

"I don't understand what you mean..."

"I found John Kirkham in Facebook..."

"Okay..."

"Send him a message. Let him know you can be on a flight leaving tomorrow afternoon..."

"Okay - Why am I doing that?"

"Let him know the flight is $1,365 – if he's not trying to scam you he'll give you his credit card or he'll offer to book your flight for you..."

"Okay – I'll do it..."

"Wait..."

"Okay..."

"Tell him he needs to pay for lodging too..."

"I don't want him to know where I'm going to be staying until I get here..."

"Good point – I'll book the Cherry Tree Cottage in Woodbridge..."

"Why are you booking a cottage for me? I don't need a cottage..." I laughed...

"Privacy..."

"Okay..."

"I'll book the cottage and I'll send the message to him..." Beautiee said as she went back to the computer...

"Hello Mr. Kirkham,

I can be on a flight leaving tomorrow afternoon leaving Hartford at 2:47 p.m. The cost of the flight is $1,365. Please let me know if you can provide me with a credit card or if you are willing to book the flight.

Thank you.

Bazil J. Osgood"

"Okay – I logged into your Facebook – I sent the message –here's your confirmation for the cottage..." she said as my confirmation printed...

"I wish you would come with me..."

"I wish I could..."

"We'll plan a trip to the UK after I come back..." I said as I tried to pull her into a kiss...

"Hold on – you got a message..." she said as she snatched up the phone and started replying...

"I'll Zelle you $1,365 – what's your phone number?"

"203-578-2798"

"Thanks – I'll send it now..."

"He sent $1,365 via Zelle – I'm gonna book your flight..." she said as she sat back at the computer.   I watched her fingers fly on the keyboard...

"How fast do you type?"

"About 70 words per minute..." she answered without looking up... "You should get confirmation in a few minutes..."

"Beautiee..."

"Yes?"

"Stop..."

"What?"

"Stop..."

"Okay..."

"Come here..."   Beautiee got up from behind the desk and stood in front of me... "Now..." I breathed as I kissed her... "I want you to relax for the rest of the day..."

"I need to..."

"What did I just tell you?"

"I need to relax for the rest of the day..."

"If you need me to remind you again..." I breathed as I kissed her... "I'll take you back upstairs..."

"Oohhh... I like the sound of that..."

"C'mon y'all..." Keisha said...

"Okay!" they all answered as they came downstairs...

"I'll be back..."

"Bye Uncle Troy!" they all said as they followed Keisha out the door...

"Mommy! Daddy!" they all exclaimed as they came inside...

"Hey – come sit in the living room – we need to talk..."

"Y'all good?" Keisha asked...

"We're okay Keisha..." Beautiee answered...

"Okay – I'll see y'all tomorrow..." she said as she started to leave...

"Keisha – wait..." I said...

"You want me to stay?"

"Yes..."

"Y'all goin' be long?"

"You in a hurry?" I laughed...

"Kinda..."

"Okay – I'll make this quick – Daddy's going on a trip tomorrow..."

"Can we go?" Lydia asked...

"Not this time..."

"When are you coming back Daddy?" Jay asked...

"I should be home in a couple of days..."

"Do we have to go to Chandler's house?"

"No Jay – you'll be here with Mommy..."

"When are you leaving?" Joseph asked...

"I'm leaving tomorrow afternoon..."

"Will you be here when we get home from school?" Joy asked...

"No..."

"Okay..." she sighed...

"I'm gonna miss you Daddy..." Lydia said...

"I'll see y'all later..." Keisha said as she got up...

"Bye Auntie Keisha!" they all said as she left...

"Mommy – what's for dinner – I'm hungry!" Jay exclaimed...

"Ask Daddy – he told me I have to relax for the rest of the day..." she laughed...

"How 'bout Chinese food?" I suggested...

"Yeeaaah!"

"Good morning..." Beautiee breathed as I kissed her awake...

"Mmm... Good morning..."

"Let's get in the shower before the kids get up...

"C'mon..." Jay said...

"I'm tired..." Lydia yawned...

"Me too..." Joy yawned...

"Me too..." Joseph yawned...

"I wish we had more time..." Beautiee whispered...

"We'll make time..." I breathed as I thrust myself inside her...

"Everybody ready?" Jay asked...

"Yes..." they all answered in unison...

"Good – let's go downstairs..."

"Are you ready Beautiee?"

"I'm ready..."

"Good – let's go downstairs." When we got downstairs the kids were all eating cereal...

"Good morning!" they all exclaimed when they saw us...

"Good morning!" we both exclaimed in unison...

"Thank you Jay..." I said...

"You're welcome Daddy. Beautiee and I watched as they cleaned the table and put the dishes in the dishwasher...

"Bye Daddy!" they all said in unison. I knelt down and held out my arms and they ran into them...

"Be good for your mother while I'm gone..."

"Yes Daddy!" they all said in unison as they ran outside to get their bus...

"Come'ere Beautiee..." I breathed as I pulled her into a hug, kissed her, and she started crying... "Beautiee... what's wrong?"

"I don't know..."

"I'll call Sam..."

"Okay..." she sniffed...

"Hey Bazil..."

"Sam – we won't be in today..."

"Everything okay?"

"I'm going to London..." I answered and then I hung up...

"Everything okay?" Joselyn asked...

"They're not coming in today..."

"They say why?"

"Bazil said he's going to London..."

"Should we tell anybody?"

"If anybody asks – I'll say he's away on business..."

"Okay..."

"Oh John..."

"Kate..."

"John... Don't Stop..."

"I won't Kate... I won't..."

"John... I'm cumming..."

"I'm cumming with you..."

"HA... HA... HA... HA.."

"UUGH... UUGH... UUGH... UUGH..."

"AAAGGGHHH!!"

"UUUGGGHHH!!"

"Good morning..." Trevor greeted...

"What the hell are you doing here?!" John snapped...

"I haven't heard from you... or your wife..."

"So you just come in uninvited?!"

"We had a deal..." John got out the bed, went over to the dresser, and checked his phone...

"Bazil will be here tomorrow morning at 6:20 a.m...."

"Where will he be staying?"

"He didn't say..."

"I'll be waiting to hear from you..."

"You can leave now..."

"Remember – you didn't see me..."

"I wish..."

"The sooner I see Bazil... the sooner you get to spend eternity with your wife..." Trevor said and then he disappeared...

"I'll be glad then this is over..." Kate sighed...

"Me too..."

"Flight 2435 to Washington now boarding at Airbus A320..."

"I'll walk you to the gate..." Beautiee said as we got up...

"Mr. Osgood – Can I get your autograph?" someone asked...

"I'm on my way to catch a plane..."

"Can I get a picture?"

"I'm sorry – I need to make sure I get to my gate on time – c'mon Beautiee!" I exclaimed as I took her by the hand and pulled her towards the gate...

"Come back to me..." Beautiee breathed as she pulled me into a kiss...

"Look! That's Bazil & Beautiee Osgood!" We continued kissing as cameras flashed...

"I will Beautiee... I promise..."

"Make sure you send an email so I can read it to the kids..."

"I'll send you a message as soon as I get to Washington..."

"I love you..."

"I love you more..." I breathed as I kissed her again and then I went to get on the plane...

Beautiee hurried out the airport to the parking garage. As soon as she got in the car she burst into tears...

"Mommy!" They all exclaimed as they came in...

"Hey..." Beautiee sighed...

"Did you hear from Daddy yet?" Jay asked...

"Not yet..."

"I'm hungry..." Joy said...

"I'll get some pizza..."

"Yeeaaah!" they all exclaimed...

"I'm going to be in the office – go upstairs and change your clothes..."

"Yes Mommy!"

"Hey My Thirst Quencher..." Beautiee sighed as she answered messenger...

"Hey..."

"Come downstairs and say good night to Daddy!" Beautiee yelled...

"Daddy!" they all exclaimed...

"Hey!"

"Are you there yet?" Jay asked...

"Not yet..."

"We had pizza Daddy!" Lydia said...

"We're being good for Mommy Daddy!" Joseph said...

"I love you Daddy!" Joy said...

"I love you all too – I'll see you soon..."

"Flight 918 for London boarding at Boeing 777..."

"That's my flight – I gotta go – I love you all..."

"We love you too Daddy..."

"I love you too Daddy..." Beautiee said...

"I love you more..." I said and then I disconnected the call...

"Beautiee..."
"Huh?" she yawned...
"Beautiee..."
"Lydia? Oh God – what's wrong?"
"It's Bazil..."
"What's wrong with Bazil? She asked as she teared up...
"He's in danger... I have to go..."
"LYDIA! COME BACK! PLEASE!" Beautiee cried...

I opened the door, walked into the foyer, picked up the greeting card, and began reading:

"We're so happy you chose the Cherry Tree Cottage to get away from it all. We value your privacy and you can rest assured you'll be able to relax without any distractions. If you need anything at all, we're just a phone call away."

"I might as well settle in..." I sighed as I opened the door... "Oh wow – I wish Beautiee was here..." I walked into the house and looked over at the fireplace... "Maybe I'll start a fire later..." I said as I looked in all the other rooms... "There's enough room for all of us... I should've brought them with me... Next time – when I'm not chasing zombies..." I laughed... "Oh well – I guess I'll go to the main bedroom..." When I got there I missed Beautiee even more... "A King-sized bed without my Queen..." I sat down on the bed, pulled out my laptop, and looked for restaurants in the area... "Hmmm – I'll ask John to meet me at The Crown after I get a nap – it's only a 9-minute walk from here..." I said as I closed my laptop, lay down, and closed my eyes...

I jumped as my cell phone rang... "This is Bazil..."

"Mr. Osgood – this is John Kirkham..."
"Hello John..."
"Are you settled in?"
"As settled as I can be without my family..."
"I'm sorry to hear that Mr. Osgood – I wish we could've met under other circumstances..."

"So do I — listen — can we meet at The Crown?"

"Sure — I can come pick you up — where are you?"

"I'm 9 minutes away — I'd like to walk..."

"9 minutes away — you must be staying at the Cherry Tree Cottage..."

"I am..."

"Okay — I'll see you in about 15 minutes..."

"Thank you John..." I got up, went outside, made sure the door was locked, and began walking... "One day we're going to be here Beautiee..." I sighed as I walked. I loved the cool air and the fall colors. When I got to the restaurant I started having second thoughts... "Oh boy..."

"Welcome to The Crown — take a seat anywhere you'd like — I'll be right over with a menu..." he said. I picked out a table in the corner facing the door so I'd see John when he came inside...

"Here you are..." he said as he brought over a menu...

"Excuse me..." I said before he walked away...

"Yes sir?"

"What's your name?"

"My name's Terrance..."

"I'm Mr. Osgood..."

"Nice meeting you Mr. Osgood — if you need anything just let me know..."

"This is an interesting menu..." I said out loud as I looked over everything... "I think I'll start out with A Pretty Pig Deal..." I laughed as I read: "Blyth burgh pork scratchings served with applesauce — what the hell is a pork scratching? Something that itches?" I continued to look over the menu and I was relieved when I found something I recognized: Air Aged Sirloin: House cut, off the bone, chips, béarnaise sauce, roasted red onion, watercress. "Perfect..." I looked under their 'Encore' section and when I saw the Blondie it reminded me of our honeymoon and I missed Beautiee even more: White chocolate Blondie with cherries and chocolate brownie ice cream. I read their selection of 'Hot Drinks' and I smiled when I saw they had Beautiee's favorite: Macchiato... "I'm going to bring you next time Beautiee... I promise..."

"Mr. Kirkham — it's great to see you!" Terrance greeted...

"I'm meeting Mr. Osgood — is he here?"

"Yes sir — come with me!" Terrance exclaimed as he brought John over to the table and I stood up...

"Mr. Osgood — thank you for coming — it's great to meet you..." he said as he grabbed my hand and shook it..."

"It's great meeting you too – please – sit down..."

"I saw you looking over the menu – do you know what you're having?" Terrance asked...

"I'll start out with A Pretty Pig Deal followed by the Air Aged Sirloin with Skin-On Fries, and for the encore I'd like the Blondie..." I answered...

"That sounds good – I'll have what he's having..." John said...

"Okay – I'll be back..." Terrance said...

"Mr. Osgood... Please don't be mad at me..."

"Why would I be mad at you?"

"I wasn't completely honest in my letter..."

"What do you mean?"

"Well... How can I say this..."

"Say it like a man..."

"Okay – I don't want you to help me send my wife back to the afterlife..."

"Is your wife dead?"

"Oh yes – I wouldn't like about that..."

"So what are you lying about?"

"I want you to kill me..."

"WHAT?!"

"Mr. Osgood – Please – Don't leave – Just hear me out..."

"Here's your Pretty Pigs..." Terrance said as he put them on the table... "What are you drinking tonight?"

"Ginger ale..." I answered...

"Okay – I'll be back..."

"John – I can't do that – I'm sorry..."

"I don't want you to do it – I want you to watch me do it..."

"You mean you want me to assist you with your own suicide?"

"Yes..."

"John – I have to ask – Why would you want to do this?" I started eating as Terrance put the ginger ales on the table and walked away...

"Mr. Osgood – I fell in love with my wife as soon as I saw her..."

"I know the feeling..."

"When she died – I fell into a deep depression – I've thought about suicide everyday..." he said as he started to tear up...

"You okay John?" Terrance asked as he put our sirloins on the table...

"I'm okay..." John answered as he dabbed his eyes...

"What changed?" I asked as I cut into the sirloin...

"I found the Tales on Tuesdays Book Club..."

"I see..."

"They saved my life – especially during the pandemic..."

"Really? How so?"

"We meet every Tuesday but when the pandemic started we could only meet online so we kept meeting on zoom..."

"That's nice! I'm happy you found them..."

"So am I – at least I was..."

"Was?"

"Well – I don't know how to tell you this..."

"Say it like a man..."

"More like a crazy man..." he sighed...

"John?"

"Yes Mr. Osgood?"

"Try me..."

"Okay... So... My wife's been dead for a little over a year..."

"Okay..."

"So... she started visiting me..."

"Okay..."

"Mr. Osgood?

"Yes John?"

"I'm not talking about a ghost..."

"I know..."

"So you believe me?"

"Yes John – I believe you..."

"So... the first time I woke up because... I can't even say it..."

"John – It's okay..."

"My wife and I had a great sex life..."

"Okay..."

"And now that she's dead..."

"John?"

"Yes Mr. Osgood?"

"You've been having sex with your dead wife – haven't you?"

"Yes..."

"Have you told anyone else about this?"

"Well... I told Claire..."

"Who's Claire?"

"She started the book club..."

"Ooohhh..."

"They all think I'm crazy!"

"You're not crazy..."

"Thank you! I thought I was until I saw your story..."

"You saw my story?"

"News travels in the UK just like any other place in the world..."

"Oh wow..."

"Once we saw how to treat the area the government invested in the weed killer but there's a problem..."

"What's the problem?"

"Sutton Hoo is a Royal Sacred Burial Ground – royal sacred burial grounds can't be disturbed..."

"So the zombies are allowed to live and love in sacred burial grounds..."

"Yes..."

"Was your wife buried there?"

"Yes..."

"How does your wife come to you?"

"There's a spot in my backyard nobody knows about..." John whispered...

"So your wife came up in your backyard... and you brought her in the house?"

"Yes..."

"And then when she leaves the same way she came?"

"Yes..."

"Ready for your Blondies?" Terrance asked...

"Yes Sir!" I exclaimed...

'Okay – I'll be right back!" Terrance exclaimed as he cleared our dishes from the table...

"I can take you to her..."

"You can? Why?"

"I want you to see her..."

"You really love her..."

"Yes..."

"What if it doesn't work?"

"I've already told her what I want to do – she'll make sure I find her..."

"Here's Blondies!" Terrance exclaimed as he put them on the table...

"Mr. Osgood – are you okay?"

"I miss my wife..." I sighed as we started eating dessert and Terrance put the check on the table...

"I'll take that..." John said...

"John – that's okay..."

"Mr. Osgood – you've done more than enough – please – let me do this for you..."

"Okay..." We finished our dessert and John got up first...

"Okay John – where are we going?"

"We're going to my car..."

"Okay..." I said as I followed him outside. We rode for about 15 minutes without speaking... "Where are we?"

"We're at Piccadilly Circus..."

"Piccadilly Circus?"

"Yes..."

"Are we back in Westminster?"

"Yes..."

"I thought we were going to Sutton Hoo?"

"We are – I just wanted to take you on a tour of downtown..."

"Oh so this is downtown?"

"Yes..."

"Why do they call it Piccadilly Circus?"

"According to Google, in 1612 a man named Robert Baker built a mansion just north of here. He got rich selling piccadills..."

"What's a piccadill?"

"A piccadill is a stiff collar the gents wear incourt..."

"Oh... okay..."

"Mr. Baker's mansion was nick-named Piccadilly Hall, so the name stuck..."

"So Piccadilly Circus is famous..."

"It's London's most famous square..."

"Why is it called a circus?"

"According to Wikipedia, circus is from the Latin word meaning circle – a round open space at a street junction..."

"I had no idea..." I began to relax a bit and enjoyed the billboards and bright lights as we road past the theatres. I got excited when I saw the Apollo... "Hey! Apollo Theatre!"

"Just like New York City..." John said. We continue riding past Camden Town, Big Ben, and Buckingham Palace...

"Oh wow..."

"Beautiful – Isn't it?"

"I can't wait to bring my wife here..." I sighed as it started getting dark...

"Have you done any research on Sutton Hoo?"

"I know about the Burial Mounds, The Great Ship, The Prince and His Horse, and viewing the Royal Burial Ground from above..."

"We're going to go to the Tower now..."

"Isn't it past viewing hours?"

"Yes..."

"So how are we going to see your wife?"

"She usually comes out from behind the tower at this time..."

"Does she know I'm coming?" John sighed before he answered...

"I told my wife you were coming..."

"That's okay... I guess..."

"They can't leave the burial ground so we'll be fine..."

"How long have you been coming here after hours?"

"About three weeks..." he answered as he parked the car. When we got behind the tower I didn't see anyone at first... "There..."

CHAPTER 9

"Oh my God..." I whispered as I teared up. John had no idea why I was so emotional...

"That's my wife..." I was in shock and awe at the same time. I watched and cried as his wife danced around with my parents. I was so caught up in the moment I didn't notice Trevor watching me...

"John? John – is that you?"

"It's me my love..." John said as he stood up...

"Bazil..." my mother whispered...

"Mom..." I cried...

"Come here Son..." my father said as he held open his arms...

"I can't..."

"Yes you can – they won't hurt you..." John breathed as he ran to his wife. I watched them embrace as zombies were fucking a couple of feet from them...

"Come to me..." my father said. I ran to my father, threw my arms around him, and cried... "I love you Son..."

"Dad... How are you alive?" I cried...

"Bazil..." my mother sighed as she pulled me into a hug and I cried even harder...

"Oh my God... Mom..."

"I never thought I'd be holding you again..."

"I miss Beautiee..." I cried. I had no idea that Trevor was watching us...

"Bazil – this is my wife, Kate..."

"Thank you for coming Mr. Osgood..." she said as she pulled me into a hug...

"You're welcome – these are my parents..."

"Bazil & Lydia are your parents? Oh Wow!"

"Thank you John for asking me to come out here..."

"Yes John... Thank you for asking Bazil to come out here..." Trevor whispered...

"Now that you've met my wife – what do you think?" John asked...

"I can't do it..." I answered...

"Can't do what?" my father asked...

"I contacted your son to ask him to help me get my wife back to the afterlife – but the truth is I want your son to help me join my wife in the afterlife..."

"You want my son to kill you?" my mother asked...

"Yes..."

"Are you okay with this?" my mother asked Kate...

"I wasn't at first. I wanted John to move on and be happy – even if that meant I'd be miserable..."

"This defies the natural order of things..." my father said...

"Mr. Osgood – I mean no disrespect – but I'm desperate – I didn't know what else to do..."

"But you knew to contact my son..."

"Everyone else thinks I'm crazy..."

"I'm dead – and I think you're crazy!" my father laughed...

"Bazil stop it – you should understand how he feels better than anybody..." my mother said...

"I understand how you feel..." I said...

"You're just saying that..." John sighed...

"If I didn't understand how you were feeling I wouldn't be here..."

"I wish I could just bite you and turn you into a zombie!" Kate exclaimed...

"That's not what happens when you bite me..." John laughed...

"Oh my God! You've been fucking your wife!" my father exclaimed...

"Yes... he has..." Kate sighed...

"Now I understand..." my father said...

"Finally!" John exclaimed...

"You're addicted..."

"I'm addicted?'

"The first time we made love after we found each other it was explosive..."

"It definitely was..." my mother added...

"Oh wow!" Kate exclaimed...

"In the afterlife – You don't have to get in the mood – you don't have to get turned on – you just are – and when you find the love of your life – they are – and it's explosive..."

"So... I'm going to get worse after I die?" John asked...

"It's not worse – it's better – trust me..." my father answered...

"So... I'm an addict?"

"I'm afraid so..." my father answered...

"I'm addicted to my wife..." John breathed as he kissed her...

"Oh John..." she moaned...

"Okay that's it – break it up..." my father laughed as he pushed them apart...

"Bazil – you need to go..." my mother said...

"Mom – I..."

"BAZIL – YOU NEED TO GO!"

"Let's go..." I sighed as I turned to walk away...

70

"Did I do something?" John asked...

"GO!" my mother commanded...

"Okay... I'll go..."

"I love you John..." Kate sighed...

"I love you too..."

"I'm going to sit over there..." Kate sighed as she left my parents standing where they were...

"Mi Lydia, ¿qué pasa?"

"Nuestro hijo está en peligro..."

"¿De quien?"

"Trevor..."

"¿Trevor? ¿Él está aquí?"

"Sí..."

"¿Está seguro?"

"Puedo sentirlo..."

"Mi Lydia – what's wrong?"

"Our son is in danger..."

"From who?"

"Trevor..."

"Trevor? He's here?"

"Yes..."

"Are you sure?"

"I can feel him..." my mother answered as my father pulled her into his arms and held her as she trembled...

"I'll see you soon..." Trevor breathed as he watched us drive off...

CHAPTER 10

"Thank you for asking me to come out here..."

"You're not mad?"

"If it weren't for you – I wouldn't've seen my parents...

"I can't believe my wife was dancing with your parents..."

"Your wife is very sweet..."

"Can I ask you something?"

"I'm not going to change my mind..."

"I know – that's not what I wanted to ask you..."

"What do you need to ask me?"

"Since you won't do it – If I don't do it – how long can we stay as we are?"

"I have no idea..." I sighed. We rode the rest of the way in silence. As happy as I was to see my parents, I was wishing I was home. I had no idea what was going to happen next and I kept hearing my mother telling me I needed to go...

"We're here..."
"Thank you John..."
"You're welcome..."
"Good night John..."
"Can I call you tomorrow?"
"Sure John – you can call me tomorrow..." I answered as I got out the car and went inside...

"Beautiee..." I sighed as I went into the bedroom, sat on the bed, and laid back... "I wish you were here..." I sighed as I closed my eyes, took my dick out my pants, and began stroking it...

"Oh shoot – Bazil left his cell phone – I need to bring this to him!" John exclaimed as he turned the car around and headed back to the cottage...

"Is everyone ready?" Trevor asked. The zombies nodded their head in agreement... "Okay – let's do this..." Trevor growled as he opened the door and came inside with the zombies following behind him...

"BAZIL – NECESITAMOS IR – ¡NUESTRO HIJO ESTÁ EN PELIGRO!"
"¡¿DONDE ESTA EL?!"

"ÉL ESTÁ EN LA CABAÑA – ¡¡DEBEMOS DARNOS PRISA!!"

"BAZIL – WE NEED TO GO – OUR SON'S IN DANGER!"

"WHERE IS HE?!"

"HE'S AT THE COTTAGE – WE NEED TO HURRY!!"

"Beautiee......" I moaned. My eyes were closed and I imagined Beautiee sucking my dick as I was getting close to cumming. I had no idea Trevor was standing over me...

"Bazil... I've missed you..."

"Trevor?"

"Yeesss..." he breathed as he got on the bed on his knees, got between my legs, and took my dick in his mouth...

"Trevor... Shit..."

"Yesss Daddy..." Trevor breathed as he took my dick in his mouth again all the way down to my balls...

"TREVOR... FFUUCCKK!!"

"Was it good Daddy?"

"Yes Trevor... Yes..." I breathed and then Trevor got up off the bed...

"Trevor – how did you know I'd be here?"

"We followed you from the burial ground..."

"We?" I asked as I tried to get up but I couldn't move. Zombies had me pinned down on the bed...

"TURN HIM OVER!" Trevor commanded...

"Trev..." I tried to talk but I was no match for them. I knew what Trevor was up to when I was pinned down on my stomach as the zombies ripped my clothes off my body and spread my legs apart... "Trevor..." I pleaded... "What are you doing?"

"I'M GOING TO FUCK YOU TO DEATH – AND THEN YOU'LL BE MINE FOR ETERNITY! AAHHH HHAA HHAA HAA!!" I teared up as I thought about Beautiee and Trevor got on top of me. I braced myself as he spread my cheeks and I felt the tip of his dick... "AAAAHHHH!!"

"LET MY SON GO!!" my father commanded. The zombies let go of me, I turned on my back, and I pushed myself up as Trevor turned towards my father, pulled the lamp my father shoved inside his body out, and threw it on the floor...

"I'LL KILL YOU!!" Trevor growled as he lunged for my father and they began fighting...

"UUGH!! UUGH!! UUGH!! UUGH!! UUGH!!"

"BAZIL – LOOK OUT!!" my mother screamed. I jumped up off the bed and tried to get to my mother but Trevor beat me to her, grabbed her arms, and held them behind her back. The zombies stood around the room, waiting for instructions...

"You do what the fuck I tell you – or I'll rip her fuckin' arms off!" he gritted...

"Please... I'll do anything you want..." my father pleaded...

"Bazil... come to me..." Trevor commanded as he turned his back to me and started backing out of the room with my mother in front of him...

"Trevor... Please... Don't hurt my mother... I'll come to you..." I pleaded as I got up off the bed and began walking towards Trevor as John picked up the lamp and shoved it in his head from behind...

"AAAAHHHH!!" Trevor dropped dead and the zombies that came with him dropped dead around the room...

"Dad..."

"BAZIL – GO HOME!!" my father commanded as he pulled my mother towards the window...

"WAIT!! TAKE ME WITH YOU!! PLEASE!!" John pleaded...

"ARE YOU SURE THIS IS WHAT YOU WANT?!" my father asked...

"YES!!"

"COME TO ME!!" my father commanded. John walked over to my father and tossed my cell phone on the bed. I watched as my father grabbed John's head with both hands and held his head. John went limp and my father picked him up in his arms...

"Dad..."

"Go home..."

"I love you..."

"We love you too..." my mother said. My parents walked through the wall with John and I cried.

"Oh my God – I don't know what to do first..."

"Put some clothes on..." God commanded...

"Huh?"

"I said put some clothes on..."

"Umm... Okay – I'll put some clothes on..." I said as I opened my suitcase, took out some clothes, and got dressed... "I'm dressed..."

"I can see that..."

"Oh my God – you saw us..."

"Bazil – you don't have time for that – pick up the torn clothes and put them in the garbage..." I did as I was told, sat on the bed, and waited...

"Drag the bodies outside..."

"Won't they be seen by the owner?"

"They'll be dust before the owner gets back..." I pulled the zombies outside one by one. When I pulled the last one outside, I looked at the pile and started counting...

"One, two, three, four, five..."

"Bazil – get your things and go..." I went back in the house, grabbed my suitcase, and left the bedroom..."

"You forgot your phone..." I hurried back inside, put my phone in my pocket, and hurried outside...

"Oh my God! How am I going to get to the airport?"

"Take John's car..."

"I don't have any keys!"

"The keys are in the ignition..."

"Thank you Lord! Thank you!"

"You're welcome..."

"Oh my God – John!" Kate exclaimed... "What happened?!"

"I gave him what he wanted..." my father answered...

"So he's dead?"

"He's dead..."

"John? John! Wake up! Why won't he answer me?!"

"I don't know..."

"Johnnn! Please come back to meeee!"

"Go sit down..." my father commanded. Kate went to sit behind the tower as my father and mother followed...

"Okay – I'm sitting..."

"Hold out your arms..." Kate held out her arms and my father placed John in her arms. It was awkward for her so my father helped Kate cradle him like a baby...

"Is my husband ever going to wake up?" Kate asked as she teared up...

"I have no idea..." my father answered as he took my mother's hand and they walked away...

"Bazil, mi amor, ¿estás bien?"

"No..."

"Bazil está bien..."

"Bazil no debería haber venido…"

"Él quería ayudar..."

"Debería haberlo matado en lugar de ayudarlo..."

"Bazil… No… No fue su culpa…"

"Estuvimos tan cerca de perder a nuestro hijo..."

"Bazil... Mi amor... Trevor iba a seguir intentándolo hasta llegar a nuestro hijo... no fue culpa de John..."

"Si John no se acercó a él..."

"Mi amor, si no fuera John, habría sido otra persona…"

"Mi Lydia, ¿cómo sabes esto?"

"John no tenía idea de lo que iba a pasar, lo único de lo que John era culpable era de enamorarse de su esposa... otra vez..."

"Mi Lydia – Te quiero mucho..."

"Yo también te amo..."

"Si supiera que Trevor estaba aquí..."

"Lo sé mi amor... lo sé..."

"Bazil – my love – are you okay?"

"No..."

"Bazil is okay..."

"Bazil shouldn't've come..."

"He wanted to help..."

"I should've killed John instead of helping him..."

"Bazil... No... It wasn't his fault..."

"We came so close to losing our son..." my father whispered as he teared up...

"Bazil... My love... Trevor was going to keep trying until he got to our son... it wasn't John's fault..."

"If John didn't reach out to him..."

"My love – if it wasn't John – it would've been someone else..."

"My Lydia – how do you know this?"

"John had no idea what was going to happen – the only thing John was guilty of was falling in love with his wife... again..."

"Mi Lydia – I love you so much..." my father breathed as he kissed her...

"I love you too..."

"If I knew Trevor was here..." he gritted...

"I know my love... I know..."

"Mr. Osgood..." John said as he approached my father...

"I don't want to talk to you..." my father said...

"Mr. Osgood... Please..." Kate pleaded...

"John – you got what you wanted – and my son nearly paid with his life – please go – I don't want or need to see either of you ever again..."

"I'm sorry..." John whispered...

"You saved my son's life – and I'll never forget that – but you also put my son in danger – and I'll never forget that either..."

"C'mon John..." Kate sighed as she took his hand and led him back to the tower...

"I wish I never listened to Trevor..." John sighed... "He didn't give a damn about me – he just used me to get Mr. Osgood to come out here – what if I didn't get there in time?!"

"So that's what Mr. Osgood meant..."

"Mr. Osgood left his phone in my car so I went back there to bring him his phone..."

"John – that was God..."

"Don't say that..."

"Don't you see? Mr. Osgood left his phone in your car... you had to bring him his phone... you had to be there... you had to kill Trevor... Trevor reaped his Karma..."

"Oh my God... Kate..." John cried...

"Yes John..." she cried as they started kissing. They couldn't control their urges as they fell down on the ground... "John..."

"Kate..."

"John..."

"Kate..." John opened Kate's blouse and began kissing her breasts...

"Oh John..." John pushed his pants off his body as Kate held him against her...

"JOOOHHHNNN!" she moaned as he thrust himself inside her... "OOOHHH!!"

"AAAGGGHHH!!"

"OOOHHH!!"

"AAAGGGHHH!!"

"OOOHHH!!"

"AAAGGGHHH!!"

"OOOHHH!!"

"AAAGGGHHH!!"

"OOOHHH!!"

"AAAGGGHHH!!" The other zombies stopped what they were doing, stood up, and turned towards the tower...

"BAZIL – LOOK!!" my mother exclaimed as she pointed towards the tower and my father smiled... "Why are you smiling?" my mother asked...

"Welcome to the afterlife John..." my father sighed...

I pulled out my phone and went to expedia.com to look for flights... "God please let there be a flight tonight..."

"There is..."

"Oh thank God – there's one left – I'm going to book it right now!" I exclaimed as I clicked on it... "Shit – it's $1,600 – oh well – it's worth it to get home to Beautiee..." I said as I looked up at the GPS and saw a gold American express card and an envelope addressed to Claire... "Thank you John..." I said as I booked the flight... "Shit – It's 8:30 – I'm cutting it close!"

"You'll make it Bazil – Go!" God commanded as I began speeding. When I got to the red light I stopped to look at the notification and saw that I received my confirmation email... "I'm on my way home Beautiee!" I exclaimed as I drove...

I got to the airport at 9:30... "You're just in time Mr. Osgood..."

"Thank you..."

"Will you be checking your bag?"

"No..." I answered as I grabbed my tickets and hurried to the gate just as they were about to board...

"Flight Turkish Airlines 1984 to Istanbul now boarding..." I got in line, got on the plane, and sat down...

"Mr. Osgood?" the flight attendant asked as she approached me...

"Yes?"

"Can I get your autograph?" she asked as she handed me a copy of Beautiee's Autobiography...

"Sure..." I smiled as I opened the book and signed it...

"Thank you!" she exclaimed as she hurried off down the aisle. Thank God no one else recognized me because I wasn't in the mood for talking – I needed to close my eyes and sleep – or try to anyway...

"Hey..." someone said as they shook me... "Are you okay?"

"I was sleeping..."

"You were having a nightmare..."

"Sorry if I disturbed you..."

"That's okay – I had nightmares on my first flight too..."

"Ladies and Gentlemen we'll be arriving at Istanbul shortly. Please return to your seats and faster your seatbelts...

"Oh thank God – I can't wait to get off this plane and stretch my legs!" he said. I acknowledged him by nodding and looked the other way...

"Where can I get a cup of coffee?" I asked a he approached me...

"There's a Starbucks over there..." he pointed out...

"Thanks..." I said as I started to get up and his wife ran up to him...

"Honey! You didn't tell me you were with Bazil Osgood!"

"Bazil Osgood? Oh my God! I had no idea!"

"Hello..." I greeted...

"I'm Ken and this is my wife, Kathy..."

"Nice to meet you both..."

"Listen – I'd love to get a quick interview..." he said as he took out a pad and pen...

"No thank you..."

"Mr. Osgood – I'll be quick – just a couple of questions..."

"Honey – he said no..." his wife said...

"Can I get a picture?"

"Sure..." I answered as I stood up and he pulled out his phone to take a selfie...

"Kate – get in the picture..."

"Okay!" she squealed as she jumped up, hugged me, and Ken took the picture...

"Thank you Mr. Osgood – here's my card – call me so we can schedule that interview..."

"Okay..." I said as I took the card. I was relieved when they left... "Where's the bathroom?" I asked as I looked around. I found the bathroom, went inside, threw his card in the garbage, and stood in line. I went into the next stall, took my dick out to pee, and pissed all over the seat as I began to shake uncontrollably...

"Oh my God... Why is this happening to me?!" I cried...

"Are you okay in there Sir?" somebody asked as they banged on the door...

"I'll be out in a sec..." I answered as I shook my dick, put it back in my pants, zipped up my zipper, cleaned off the seat, and came out the stall...

"Are you okay?" security asked...

"I'm okay – thanks for checking on me..."

"You're welcome..." I washed my hands, threw some water on my face, dried off, and left the bathroom. I stood in line at Starbucks and got a cup of coffee. After I got a cup of coffee I found a bench, sat down, and opened my laptop. The first email I sent was to Beautiee:

"Hey Beautiee,

I had a horrible night. I wish you were here with me but at the same time, I'm glad you weren't. I left Westminster last night. I arrived at Istanbul at 4 a.m. But my flight doesn't leave until 3:05 this afternoon so I'm going to try and get some work done. I'll let you know where I am when I get there. I tried to sleep on the plane but I woke up another passenger because I was having a nightmare so I probably won't be getting sleep anytime soon. I broke down in the men's room earlier and I haven't been okay since. I'm in a very dark place and I don't know how long it will be before I'm okay. Please don't call me because as soon as I hear your voice, I'll break down and I won't be able to stop crying.

Love, Bazil"

"Good morning..." Beautiee greeted as she walked into the office...
"Good morning Mrs. Osgood..."
"Good morning..." the employees greeted as she walked past them and went into our office...
"Good morning Mrs. Osgood..."
"Please call me Beautiee Sam..."
"Good morning Beautiee..."
"Good morning Mrs. Osgood..." Joselyn greeted as she came in...
"Good morning Joselyn..."
"I'll get you your coffee..." she said as she went to get Beautiee's coffee...
"When is Bazil coming back?" Sam asked...
"He's due back tomorrow..."
"Okay – I'll talk to you later. Sam left the office and Beautiee sat down, opened her laptop, and logged into her email...
"Bazil..." she sighed as she opened the email I sent her and began reading...

"Hey Beautiee,

I had a horrible night. I wish you were here with me but at the same time, I'm glad you weren't. I left Westminster last night. I arrived at Istanbul at 4 am. But my flight doesn't leave until 3:05 this afternoon so I'm going to try and get some work done. I'll let you know where I am when I get there. I tried to sleep on the plane but I woke up another passenger because I was having a nightmare so I probably won't be getting sleep anytime soon. I broke down in the men's room earlier and I haven't been okay since. I'm in a very dark place and I don't know how long it will be before I'm okay. Please don't call me because as soon as I hear your voice, I'll break down and I won't be able to stop crying.

Love, Bazil"

"Bazil... Nooo..." she whispered as she started crying and Joselyn came in...
"Mrs. Osgood – I have your coffee – Oh my God – what happened?!"
"I can't talk about it..."
"You need me to leave?"
"Please..." Beautiee sniffed...
"Okay..."
"Joselyn?"
"Yes Mrs. Osgood?"
"Thanks for the coffee..."
"You're welcome..." Joselyn said as she closed the door and Beautiee continued to cry...

"What happened?!" Sam asked when he saw Joselyn...

"She said she can't talk about it..." Joselyn answered as she teared up...

"Beautiee?!"

"Yea..."

"She still in the office?"

"Yea..."

"I'ma go check on her..."

"Sam... No..."

"You want me to stay here with you?"

"Please..." she pleaded with tears in her eyes...

"She'll be alright..." Sam said as he pulled Joselyn into his arms and held her...

"I don't know what to do..."

"Nothing..."

"Nothing?"

"Remember when Bazil was in a comma?"

"Yes..."

"Beautiee came to work every day and held it down..."

"She sure did..."

"If she can get through that – she'll get through whatever this is..."

"You always know what to say when I need to hear it..." she sighed...

"That's God speaking to you through me..."

"I love you Mr. Logan..."

"I love you to Mrs. Logan..."

"Well good morning!" Sheila greeted as she interrupted their kiss...

"Okay that's it – we gon' start lockin' our door like they do..." Sam laughed...

"As long as you're working on my grandchild you can lock all the doors you want!" Sheila exclaimed as she left Joselyn's office and closed the door behind her...

"Sam! Why'd you tell her that?" Joselyn laughed...

"Cause I knew it would work..." Sam breathed as he pulled Joselyn into a kiss...

Beautiee sat in quiet and did what she could to try and take her mind off what she read earlier... "Lord... Please bring my husband home..."

"He's on his way..." God said as she got a notification of another email...

"Bazil..." she sighed as she opened it and began reading...

"Hey Beautiee,

I'll be boarding the plane for Washington in a few minutes. I had some coffee and I had a cheeseburger. Thank God for Starbucks and Wendy's. I'll be in Washington at 7:15 p.m. I'm a little bit better than I was but I'm still not good. I'll email you again when I get closer.

Love, Bazil"

"Okay that's it – I'm going home..." Beautiee said as she called Joselyn on the intercom...

"Yes Mrs. Osgood?"

"Joselyn – I'm leaving for the day..."

"Have a good night..."

"You too..." she said as she hung up, got up, and left the office...

"Mommy!" they all exclaimed when they saw her...

"Auntie Beautiee!" Amina exclaimed. They all ran to her and Beautiee felt better as she hugged them...

"Hey Beautiee..." Keisha said...

"Hey..."

"What's wrong?"

"Nothing..."

"You miss Bazil..."

"Yea..."

"When's he coming home?"

"He'll be home tonight..."

"Tonight?! Girl – you should be smiling!"

"You're right – I should be..." she said as she turned to go in the house...

"Mommy – can we have pizza?" Lydia asked as Beautiee opened the door...

"Can I come over?" Amina asked...

"Yes and yes..." Beautiee laughed...

"Bye Ma!" Amina squealed as she went inside with them and Beautiee closed the door...

"Hey Keisha – where's Mina?"

"She went next door..."

"What's wrong?"

"I don't know..."

"Watchu mean you don't know?"

"Bazil's coming home tonight..."

"That's good..."

"I don't think so..."

"Why? What happened?!"

"I asked Beautiee if she missed Bazil – She said yea – I asked her when Bazil was coming back – She said tonight – I said girl you should be smiling – she gon' say you're right – I should be – and then she went in the house..."

"Oh shit..."

"Let's go upstairs..."

"You wanna go upstairs? Now?" Keisha went over to Troy, snatched him by his collar, got in his face, and kissed him hard...

"Did I stutter mutha fucka?" Troy picked Keisha up in his arms and carried her upstairs...

CHAPTER 13

"Thank you Mommy!" they all exclaimed as they ate...

"Thank you Auntie..." Amina said...

"Mommy – eat some pizza!" Lydia exclaimed. Beautiee took a slice and began eating; trying her best to fight the queasiness she was feeling. The kids went upstairs to play and Beautiee went into the living room to watch television as she waited anxiously for another notification... and fell asleep...

The sound woke her up and Beautiee snatcher her phone...

"Bazil..." she sighed as she read the email...

"Hey Beautiee..."

I'll be boarding the flight to Hartford in a few minutes. I'll be arriving in Hartford at 11:57 p.m. Please don't wake the kids if they're already sleeping. I'll be getting home late. If you can't wait up for me don't worry about it – I'll wake you up when I get home.

Love, Bazil"

Beautiee smiled to herself and got up... "I'll see you soon My Thirst Quencher..." she sighed as she went upstairs...

"Hey Beautiee – you want me to come get Amina?" Keisha asked as she answered the phone...

"She can stay – I haven't seen or heard from them since we had pizza..."

"Damn – that's good!"

"Sure was – I had a nice nap..."

"You hear from Bazil?"

"Yea..."

"He's on his way home?"

"Yea..."

"Okay – call me if you need anything – but I hope you don't need anything..."

"Bye Keisha!" Beautiee laughed as she hung up..."

"What's this?" Claire sighed as she opened her messenger... "Why am I getting a message from Bazil Osgood?" she asked as she opened the message and began reading...

"Hello Claire,

I met with John Kirkham last night. His car is in the parking lot at the airport in London. On the dashboard are his gold American Express card and an envelope addressed to you.

Sincerely,

Bazil J. Osgood"

"Oh my God! John! What did you do?!" she cried as she jumped up, hurried downstairs, and jumped in a taxi...

"Who is it?!" Donna snapped as she came downstairs...
"It's Claire!"
"Claire – what's wrong?!"
"I need you to run a DMV check!" Claire exclaimed as she came inside...
"This couldn't wait until tomorrow?!"
"No..." Claire answered as she started crying...
"Claire..." Donna whispered as she pulled her into a hug... "What's wrong?"
"He did it!"
"Who?"

"John!!"

"What did John Do?!"

"He's dead!!"

"No!!" Donna exclaimed as she started crying too... "Are you sure?"

"Here..." Claire said as she showed Donna her phone and Donna started reading the message...

"Hello Claire,

I met with John Kirkham last night. His car is in the parking lot at the airport in London. On the dashboard are his gold American Express card and an envelope addressed to you.

Sincerely,

Bazil J. Osgood"

"Oh my God... John..."

"I need you to run a DMV check so I can find his car..."

"What are we going to do when we find his car?"

"Pray his keys are in there so we can move it..." Claire answered as Donna got on the computer...

"My Thirst Quencher..." Beautiee breathed as she threw her arms around me and kissed me...

"Hey..." I sighed...

"Let's go upstairs..." Beautiee whispered as she took my hand...

"Beautiee... wait..."

"What's wrong?" she asked as she teared up...

"I need to go upstairs..." I sighed... "And I need to sleep in the guest room..."

"Why?" Beautiee began to cry and it broke my heart...

"Beautiee... please... I can't... I'm sorry..." I whispered as I cried...

"C'mon..." Beautiee sniffed as she took my hand and led me upstairs. We walked toward the bedroom and I dreaded going in there but I was relieved when we kept walking towards the guest room...

"Good night Beautiee... I love you..." I breathed as I kissed her...

"Good night My Thirst Quencher... I love you too..." Beautiee stood there and watched me close the door. I heard her crying and I slid down on the floor, held my legs and knees together, and sobbed like a baby...

"Okay – all we have to do is look for a blue 2022 Mitsubishi Mirage..." Donna said as they got in the taxi...

"How in the world are we gonna find his car?" Claire asked...

"Think like John..." Donna answered...

"Think Like John?"

"John said whenever he parks at the airport he always parks as close to the gate as he can get..."

"You're right!" Claire exclaimed... "All we need to do is find out what gate the flights leave from going back to Hartford – we'll find his car!"

"Good evening – how may I help you?"

"Good evening – could you tell me what gate the flight is leaving from going to Hartford, Connecticut?" Claire asked...

"Hhmmm... I'm sorry Maam – we don't have any flights going to Hartford until tomorrow..."

"Did you have a flight yesterday at around 10 p.m.?"

"Hmmm... Let me see... Yes – that flight left at 10:10 p.m..."

"What gate did it leave from?"

"It says here it left from Airbus A321..."

"Which way is Airbus A321?" Donna asked...

"Did you need to report something lost or stolen?"

"I'm sorry..." Claire sighed... "My friend asked me to pick up his car for him – I was supposed to be here last night but I overslept..."

"I see – that happens from time to time – Airbus A321 is down the corridor to the right..."

"Thank you!" they both exclaimed in unison as they ran towards the gate...

"Parking lot straight ahead!" Donna exclaimed...

"I see it – Go!" Claire exclaimed as they pushed the door open...

"There it is!" Donna exclaimed as they ran over to the car and Donna snatched the door open...

"Excuse me – is this your car?" the security officer asked...

"It's my husband's car..." Claire answered as she got in the driver's seat...

"You got here just in time – I was just about to write you a ticket!" he said before he walked away...

"God that was close!" Donna exclaimed...

"Here's the card..." Claire breathed as she put it in her pocket... "And here's the envelope!" she exclaimed as she held it up...

"Oh my God – read it!"

"I'll read it when we get back to your place – let's get the hell out of here!" Claire exclaimed as she started the car, put it in drive, and left the airport...

"Daddy!" they exclaimed when they saw me...

"Uncle Bazil!" Amina exclaimed...

"Hey..." I sighed as I bent down to hug them and they ran towards me...

"Where's Mommy?" Lydia asked...

"I'm right here..." Beautiee sighed. Beautiee smiled but I could tell she'd been crying and it made me sad...

"What's wrong Daddy?" Jay asked...

"I got in late last night – I'm still tired...

"C'mon – I'll make breakfast – and I'll make Daddy some coffee..." Beautiee said...

"Can we have pancakes?" Jay asked...

"Not today..." Beautiee sighed...

"Why not Mommy?" Joseph asked...

"Daddy makes them better than I do – and he's tired..." Beautiee answered as she went downstairs. The kids followed behind her and I had to compose myself before I could join them...

"Open it!" Donna exclaimed...

"I am!" Claire exclaimed as she opened the envelope, took out John's letter, and began reading out loud...

"Hello Claire,

I know you think I'm crazy and that's okay. Now that you're reading this letter, I'm sure you know that I've joined the love of my life, Kate in the afterlife.

Please don't be angry at Mr. Osgood. He was compassionate enough to listen and he was very supportive of my transition. In fact, he was so supportive he went with me to meet my wife and he also introduced me to his parents!"

"Oh my God!" they both exclaimed and then Claire continued reading...

"My wife and I are living happily and erotically ever after at the Royal Sacred Burial Ground, Sutton Hoo. We'll be out frolicking after 8 p.m. on Saturday night. I'd love to see you. If you decide to come – I have to warn you: the zombies are oblivious to what's around them. They won't hurt you but they don't care to stop what they're doing either. Hopefully I'll see you Saturday night. If not Saturday night, perhaps another night. If you decide not to come at all, please know that I'm truly happy.

Sincerely,

John Kirkham"

"I thought it was just a myth..." Donna said...
"How did he know what the zombies were doing? How does he know they won't hurt us?" Claire asked...
"Think like John..."

"I can't!"

"Claire?"

"Yes Donna?"

"Think like John..."

"Oh my God..."

"Go on..."

"He had this planned before Mr. Osgood got here..."

"Exactly..."

"I'm going to see him..."

"I was hoping you would say that..." Donna said as she got up and went over to the computer...

"Thank you Mommy!" they all exclaimed...

"You're welcome...

"Thank you Auntie Beautiee..." Amina said...

"You're welcome...

"Thank you Beautiee..." I said...

"You're welcome – you want some more coffee?"

"Sure..."

"Okay..." she said as she took my cup and poured me some more coffee. She added the hazelnut cream and sugar, put it on the table in front of me, and turned her back to me as she began putting the dishes in the dishwasher...

"Beautiee – let me help you with that..."

"Finish your coffee – I got it..."

"Okay." I sat at the table and drank my coffee just to be near her as she continued loading the dishwasher. When she was finished, she started to leave the kitchen but I stopped her... "Beautiee... Wait..."

"Yes Bazil?"

"I love you..." I breathed as I pulled her into a kiss...

"I love you too." I left the kitchen and I could hear her crying. I started to tear up and I hurried upstairs into the guest room so I could break down behind the door...

"Mommy?"

"Yes Lydia?" Beautiee sniffed...

"Don't cry... Daddy loves you..."

"And I love you..." Beautiee said as she picked Lydia up, hugged her, and put her back down...

"Huuuu..." Lydia cried as she came into the room...

"What's wrong?" Jay asked...

"Mommy's sad..."

"I know..."

"Why is Mommy sad? I don't want Mommy to cry..."

"Mommy was crying?" Joseph asked...

"Uh huh..."

"I'm telling Starr..." Joseph said...

"No... Lydia whispered... "You'll get in trouble...

"I'll tell Starr..." Jay said...

"No... Daddy will be mad..." Joseph said...

"Daddy shouldn't make Mommy sad then..."

"Where you goin'?" Amina asked...

"C'mon..." Jay whispered as they all followed him downstairs...

"How's this?" Donna asked as she motioned for Claire to come look at the computer...

"Hello everyone,

We just found out that our dear friend, John Kirkham, passed away last night, Friday, November 4, 2022. We don't know any of the details; however, John wrote a letter and addressed it to Claire. In that letter, he expressed that he'd like us to celebrate his life at the Royal Sacred Burial Ground at Sutton Hoo tonight at 8 p.m. I know this seems a bit odd but I'm sure John has his reasons and I'd like us all to honor his request. If you're able to, please meet Claire and myself at Sutton Hoo tonight at 8 p.m. near the tower.

Love,

Donna Morfett"

"I like it..." Claire said...

"Good – 'cause I already sent it..." Donna laughed as the notifications started coming in...

"Hey Dad..." Starr answered...

"Hi Starr..."

"Hi Jay! What's wrong?"

"Daddy came home yesterday..."

"That's nice – was he on a trip?"

"Uh huh..."

"What's wrong Jay?"

"Daddy slept in the guest room..."

"Ooohhh..."

"And Lydia said Mommy was crying in the kitchen..."

"I'll talk to Daddy..."

"Okay..." Jay said as he hung up...

"What are you doing in here?" Beautiee asked as she went into the library...

"We were just looking out the window Mommy..." Joseph lied...

"You don't have windows upstairs in your room?"

"Yes Mommy – but they only show us the backyard..."

"C'mon – y'all can't play in here..." Beautiee said as she held the door open for them to leave. Beautiee noticed the phone was off the receiver and when she went to put the phone down on the receiver, she checked the last number dialed... "Starr..."

"Beautiee – you here?" Keisha asked as she came inside...

"I'm in here..."

"It sure is quiet..."

"I know..."

"I came to get Amina..."

"She can stay – she's no trouble..."

"Thank you – but Daddy wants his Mina..."

"Okay..." Beautiee laughed...

"Amina!"

"Yes Mommy?"

"C'mon – it's time to go home!"

"Okay!" she squealed as she jumped up... "Bye y'all!" she squealed as she ran downstairs... "Bye Auntie Beautiee – c'mon Mommy – let's go!!"

"Damn – Bye Beautiee!" Keisha laughed as Amina pulled her out the door...

"Hey Mina!" Troy greeted...

"I have to tell you something – but don't tell nobody – okay?"

"What happened Amina?" Keisha asked...

"C'mon – come sit with Daddy..." Troy said as he picked her up and carried her into the living room. After they sat down on the couch, Amina spoke...

"Uncle Bazil came home last night..."

"Okay..." they both acknowledged...

"He slept in the guest room..."

"How you know that?" Troy asked...

"Jay told us..."

"Oohhh" Keisha said...

"Then we had breakfast..."

"Was Bazil there?" Troy asked...

"Yes..."

"Okay..."

"After breakfast, we went back upstairs and Lydia was crying..."

"Why was Lydia crying?"

"She said her mommy was sad and she was crying..."

"Oh shit!" Keisha exclaimed...

"Jay said he was telling so..."

"What did he do Amina?" Keisha asked...

"We went in the library and Jay called Starr – are we gonna get in trouble?"

"No Mina..." Troy sighed as he pulled her into a hug...

"Are you gonna tell Auntie Beautiee?"

"No..."

"Okay..." Amina sighed as she ran upstairs to her room. Troy and Keisha just sat there looking at each other...

"Beautiee..."

"Yes Bazil?" Beautiee answered as she opened the bedroom door...

"I made dinner..."

"Okay..." she said as she came out and I pulled her into a kiss...

"I love you..."

110

"I love you too..." she sighed as she pulled away from me and went downstairs...

"Hi Mommy!" they exclaimed when she walked into the kitchen... "Daddy made spaghetti!" Lydia exclaimed...

"I love Daddy's spaghetti..." Beautiee sighed as she sat down at the table with them and smiled as I made plates. I sat down at the table and Jay spoke...

"Let's hold hands..." We all held hands.... "God, thank you for blessing this food, thank you for blessing us, and thank you for blessing Mommy and Daddy – Amen!"

"Amen!" we all said in unison. Beautiee was smiling as she was eating and laughing as Lydia was making a mess with the spaghetti...

"Hurry up! I don't wanna be late!" Donna exclaimed...

"Really Donna? John's dead – it's a little too late to say you don't wanna be late..." Claire laughed...

"Oh my God!" Donna laughed as they got out the car and went over to the tower...

"John..."
"Yes Kate..."
"John..."
"Yes Kate... Yes...."

"John – look!" John got up, helped Kate up, and began to cry... "They're here... they're all here..."

"Yes they are..." John and Kate walked to the front of the tower as members from the Tales on Tuesdays group continued to come...

"Bazil..."
"Mi Lydia..."
"Bazil... Detente..."
"Por favor, no me hagas parar..."
"Bazil – ¡mira!"
"¿Todos ellos están aquí por John?"
"Creo que sí..."

"Bazil..."
"Mi Lydia..."
"Bazil... Stop..."
"Please don't make me stop..."
"Bazil – look!" My father stood up, helped my mother up, and they both watched in amazement...
"All they all here for John?"
"I think so..." my mother answered as John and Kate went closer...

"Thank you all for coming..." John said. John waited for everyone to be quiet before he continued... "As many of you know, when my wife passed away I was devastated. I went into a deep depression and thoughts of suicide crossed my mind on a regular basis. What many of you don't know is that I shared this with Claire..." John waited for the gasps and whispers to stop before he continued... "When I was at my lowest point, my wife came to visit me. I thought I was dreaming at first, but once I realized I wasn't dreaming, I reached out to Mr. Osgood at Osgood Publications and asked him to help my wife get back to the afterlife – but the truth is I wanted him to help me get to her..." John waited for the gasps and whispers to stop before he continued... "Please don't be sad for me. As you can see, I'm extremely happy." Everyone began to applaud and my father got emotional as he and my mother watched from a distance...

"Bazil... Mi Amor... No llores..."
"Mi Lyida... Estoy llorando porque estoy feliz..."

"Bazil... My Love... Don't cry..."
"Mi Lyida... I'm crying because I'm happy..." he breathed as he pulled my mother into a kiss...

"Mrs. Corbett?"
"Yes Mr. Corbett?"
"You've been quiet all day..."
"I know..."
"What's wrong?"
"Jay called me..."

"That's nice!"

"It wasn't nice Chandler..."

"What happened?"

"Daddy went on a trip..."

"So he missed Dad?"

"No..."

"What happened?"

"Dad has been sleeping in the guest room..."

"What?! Why?!"

"I don't know – That's not all..."

"What else?"

"Lydia told Jay that Beautiee was crying..."

"Oh no – I don't like that..."

"I don't either..."

"Did you call your father?"

"No..."

"Why not?"

"I'm going to see him tomorrow at work..."

"You sure?"

"Yes – I want to talk to him in person..."

"Good idea..." Chandler breathed as he kissed Starr on her neck...

"Ooohhh... that's nice..."

"I can be nicer..." he breathed as he pushed her back down on the bed...

"Oohhh... Chandler... I love it when you're nice to me..."

CHAPTER 15

"Lord... please help me..."

"I'm here Beautiee..."

"I need my husband..."

"I know this is hard for you – but you have to be patient..."

"I've been patient!"

"When do I come?"

"I don't understand..."

"When do I come?"

"You're always on time..." Beautiee sighed...

"Do you have faith in me?"

"Yes Lord... I have faith in you..."

"I need you to trust my timing..."

"It's hard!" Beautiee cried...

"I know it's hard – but it's almost over..."

"I don't know how much more I can take..."

"I've given you everything you need..."

"Is my husband okay?"

"He will be..."

"So he's not okay..." she whispered as she started crying...

"He will be okay..."

"When?"

"That's up to him..."

"Please help him..."

"I am..."

"Lord... please help me..."

"I'm here Bazil..."

"I need my wife..."

"I know..."

"I want to be with her – but I can't!" I exclaimed as I put my head in my hands and cried...

"You'll be with her soon..."

"Soon? What does that mean?"

"You're still dealing with a lot of trauma..."

"I'm not dealing with any trauma – what happened with Trevor is over..."

"Bazil Osgood – do you know who you're talking to?"

"Yes Lord..."

"You loved Trevor and he betrayed you..."

"I deserved that..."

"When you realize you didn't deserve what happened to you...that's when you'll fully heal..."

"I married Beautiee without telling her about him..."

"Beautiee loves you and she's forgiven you... but you're not ready to forgive yourself..."

"How can I? I keep fucking up!"

"You keep messing up because you won't let go of your guilt..."

"How am I supposed to do that?"

"You told me you were sorry..."

"I am sorry..."

"You begged for my forgiveness..."

"Yes..."

"And I forgave you..."

"Thank you..."

"And Beautiee forgave you..."

"She won't forgive me this time..."

"Are you willing to walk away from her?"

"Please don't make me walk away from her – I love her – I need her – I love them all – I need them all..."

"Why would I make you walk away from the woman you prayed for me to give you?"

"You're right – I'm sorry..."

"If you want your wife – go to her and tell her that..."

"What if she doesn't want me?"

"She wants you..."

"How can I be sure she'll still want me after I tell her what happened?"

"Before you called me I was with her..."

"You were with Beautiee? Is she okay?"

"She will be…"

"So she's not okay?" I asked with tears in my eyes…

"No…"

"Please help my wife…"

"That's why I'm here…"

"How does helping me help her?"

"I'm here because your wife is praying for you…"

"Beautiee…" I whispered as I jumped up out the bed and ran to the master bedroom…

CHAPTER 16

"Beautiee..."

"Bazil? Am I dreaming?"

"You're not dreaming..." I breathed as I kissed her...

"I missed you so much it hurt..."

"Let me make it up to you..." I breathed as I took off my clothes. Beautiee stood there admiring me from head to toe and I began to push her back towards the bed. When we got to the edge of the bed, Beautiee took my hands, fell back on the bed, and pulled me down on top of her... "Beautiee... Wait..."

"Please.... My Thirst Quencher..." she pleaded as she wrapped her arms around my neck and her legs around my waist. I couldn't hold back any longer and I didn't want to...

"Beautiee..."

"Yes... My Thirst Quencher... It's been so long..."

"I know..." I breathed as I kissed her again and eased myself inside her and began thrusting..."

"Fuck me..." she moaned in my ear...

"Good night Daddy..." Jay said as he opened the door and went into the guest room... "Daddy? Where are you?" Jay looked around the room and then he turned and went down the hall...

"Is this what you want?!" I growled...

"YESS!! FUCK ME!! YESS!!" We had no idea our son was standing outside our bedroom door...

"Daddy?"

"Yes Jay?" I answered as I slowed down but didn't stop...

"I came to say good night..."

"Hold on Jay..." I sighed. Beautiee looked up at me, pleading for me not to get up... "I'm sorry..." I whispered as I got up, put on my robe, and opened the door...

"Good night Daddy..."

"Good night Jay..."

"Is Mommy sleeping?"

"Yes – Mommy's sleeping..."

"Are you going to sleep with Mommy now?"

120

"Yes..."

"Good – that makes Mommy happy..." he said as he turned to walk away and went back to his room...

"He's right..." Beautiee whispered...

"I know..." I whispered as I took off my robe... "Now..." I whispered as I got back in bed... "Where was I?"

"You were fucking me..." Beautiee breathed as she pulled me into a kiss and pushed her tongue in my mouth. I pushed her down on her back, thrust myself inside her, and picked up where I left off... "Mmmph... Mmmph... Mmmph... Mmmph... Mmmph..."

"Mmmmm... Mmmmm... Mmmmm... Mmmmm... Mmmmm..."

"Mmmph... Mmmph... Mmmph... Mmmph... Mmmph..."

"Mmmmm... Mmmmm... Mmmmm... Mmmmm... Mmmmm..."

"Mmmph... Mmmph... Mmmph... Mmmph... Mmmph..."

"Mmmmm... Mmmmm... Mmmmm... Mmmmm... Mmmmm..."

"Mmmph... Mmmph... Mmmph... Mmmph... Mmmph..."

"Mmmmm... Mmmmm... Mmmmm... Mmmmm... Mmmmm..."

"MMMPH!! MMMPH!! MMMPH!! MMMPH!! MMMPH!!"

"MMMMM!! MMMMM!! MMMMM!! MMMMM!! MMMMM!!"

"Did you tell Daddy good night?" Joseph asked...
"Yea..."
"Where was he?"
"He's sleeping with Mommy..."
"Good – that makes Mommy happy..."
"I know..."
"Good night Jay..."
"Good night Joseph..."

"I missed you so much..." Beautiee whispered as she teared up...
"Beautiee... No... Please don't cry..." I breathed as I kissed her...
"I can't help it – it hurt!"
"I didn't mean to hurt you – I'm sorry..."
"That's not what I mean..."
"You weren't hurt because I was sleeping in the guest room?"
"Yes... but..."
"Beautiee... tell me..."
"My pussy hurt..."
"WHAT?!"
"Ssshhh!!"
"I'm sorry – but you said your pussy hurt..."
"She did..."
"How?"

"It's hard to explain..."

"Try..." I said as I propped myself up on my elbow...

"You know how your balls hurt when you don't get any pussy for a while?"

"You don't have any balls!" I laughed...

"I have a clit..."

"Ooohhh..."

"And it hurts..."

"I'm sorry..."

"My pussy ached too..."

"I'm sorry..."

"It brought me back to when I was in prison..." Beautiee couldn't finish...

"Beautiee... Please don't cry..." I cried...

"I tried to be patient... I wanted to give you space... But every night I slept alone... All I could think about was when I was in prison..." she whispered as she cried...

"Beautiee... Please... I'm sorry..." I cried...

"I haven't slept alone since I got out of prison – I put on a smile but Lydia caught me crying..."

"I'm so sorry..."

"She was so sad – she told me don't cry Mommy – Daddy loves you..."

"She's right – I do love you..." I cried...

"Do you love me enough to tell me what happened?"

"Beautiee..."

"Yes?"

"I want to..."

"Tell me..."

"I'll tell you later..." I breathed as I got up and slid down between Beautiee's legs...

"Bazil – I know what you're doing..." she breathed...

"What am I doing?" I asked and then I began flicking my tongue on her clit...

"You're... doing... this... to... keep... me... quiet..."

"You couldn't be quiet if your life depended on it..." I breathed and then I dove in...

"Does it still hurt?" I breathed...

"Yeesss..."

"How can it still hurt when you just came all over my face?"

"Ask her..." Beautiee laughed...

"I'm sorry you're hurting..." I breathed as I licked her softly... "But we need to get our children ready for school..." I breathed and then I licked her again... "So I'm going to stop for now..." I breathed as I licked her again... "But I'll be back later..." I breathed as I licked her again... "And I'll kiss you... Lick you... And suck you until you feel better..."

"Oohhh... Bazil... Don't stop..."

"I have to..." I breathed as I got up...

"Daddy?"

"Coming Jay..." I said as I put my robe on and went to open the door...

"Daddy!" They all exclaimed when the say me...

"Good morning..."

"Is Mommy okay?" Lydia asked...

"I'm okay..." Beautiee sighed as she came out into the hallway...

"Mommy!" they all exclaimed...

"Good morning..." she sighed...

"Can we have pancakes?" Jay asked...

"We can do that..." I answered as I hurried past them and they began to chase me...

"We're gonna get you Daddy!" Joseph exclaimed...

"First one downstairs gets Strawberry Pancakes!" I yelled as I lept down the stairs...

"I win!" Jay exclaimed as he hurried into the kitchen...

"You all get Strawberry Pancakes..."

"Yeeaaa!" they all exclaimed as Beautiee came into the kitchen...

"Daddy – give Mommy a kiss..." Lydia said. I did as I was told and pulled Beautiee into a kiss and Lydia smiled...

"Okay Daddy – they need their breakfast so they can get to school on time..." Beautiee said as she opened the refrigerator and began taking out the strawberries, whip cream, milk, and eggs...

"Good morning!" Amina exclaimed as she came into the kitchen along with Keisha...

"Good morning y'all..." Keisha said...

"Good morning – you're just in time for strawberry pancakes..." I said...

"Mommy – can I? Please?" Amina pleaded...

"I'on care..." Keisha answered...

"Yeeaa!" they all exclaimed...

"Keisha – come with me..." Beautiee said as she got up. I watched Keisha follow Beautiee towards the library...

"What Bazil do now?" Keisha laughed...

"Me..." Beautiee sighed...

"So y'all good?"

"Girl – I don't know..."

"What's wrong?"

"Bazil hasn't talked about what happened since he got back from the UK..."

"Maybe he's tired of talking..."

"That's what I'm afraid of..."

"Oh shit..."

"He's been sleeping in the guest room since he got back from the UK..."

"The guest room? Why'd you let him do that?"

"Because I knew he needed to..."

"Wait – he needed to? What about what you need?"

"I need my husband to be okay – and he's not..."

"Damn – did you ask him what happened?"

"No..."

"Why not?"

"I need him to tell me when he's ready..."

"I hope he tells you soon..."

"So do I..."

"Bye!" they all exclaimed as they flew out the door...

"Damn – no hugs – no kisses – just bye!" Keisha laughed...

"As long as they're happy..." Beautiee sighed...

"Aiight – I'ma go – I'll see y'all later..." Keisha said as she opened the door, went out, and closed it behind her..."

"That's not like her – she usually has coffee with you after the kids leave..." I said...

"She knows I need to have coffee with my husband..."

"I'll make us some coffee..." I sighed. Beautiee sat down at the island and watched me intently as I made the coffee. I picked up one cup of coffee and put it in front of her with no problem but when I picked up the 2nd cup, my hand started shaking and I dropped it. Beautiee got up and came over to me...

"Bazil... Come here..." she sighed as she pulled me into a hug... "C'mon..." she said as she led me into the living room and we sat down on the sofa...

"Beautiee..." I whispered as I teared up. Beautiee pulled me into a kiss and I began to cry...

"I love you..."

"I'm scared..." I whispered...

"I know..." she whispered as she wiped my tears from my face... "I heard you..."

"You heard me?"

"You were talking in your sleep..."

"I missed you so much..."

"I missed you too..."

"I don't know where to start..." I sighed...

"Start from the moment you got to the Cottage..."

"I opened the door and as soon as I walked into the foyer I saw a note welcoming me to the Cherry Tree Cottage. The more I looked around, the more I missed you..."

"Aww..."

"I wanted us to go there one day... the cottage has a fireplace... there's rooms for the kids... and the main bedroom has a king-size bed..."

"That sounds nice..."

"I pulled out my laptop, I looked for restaurants in the area, and I saw a restaurant called The Crown, so when John called me I asked him to meet me there..."

"Why didn't John come pick you up?"

"He offered – but it was only 9 minutes away – I wanted to walk..."

"Sounds nice..."

"It was... I loved the cool air and the fall colors. When I got to the restaurant I started having second thoughts..."

"Why?"

"They have an interesting menu – after I looked over everything I decided to try A Pretty Pig Deal..." I laughed...

"What?" Beautiee laughed...

"Blyth burgh pork scratchings served with applesauce..."

"What the hell is a pork scratching? Something that itches?" Beautiee laughed...

"Oh my God!" I laughed... "I said the same thing!"

"Was it good?"

"It was..."

"I'll take your word for that..."

"So I continued to look over the menu and I was relieved when I saw Air Aged Sirloin: House cut, off the bone, chips, béarnaise sauce, roasted red onion, watercress...."

"You love a good steak..."

"They had desserts listed under their 'Encore' section and when I saw the Blondie it reminded me of our honeymoon... and I missed you even more..."

"Aww..."

"That's when John came in..."

"Is he – I mean was he nice?"

"Very..."

"So far, it sounds like everything was going good..."

"It was... And then John told me the real reason he invited me there..."

"I don't understand..."

"He told me he didn't want me to help send his wife back to the afterlife – he wanted me to kill him..."

"Oh my God!"

"I told him I couldn't do it and he said he didn't want me to do it – he wanted me to watch him kill himself..."

"So he wanted you to assist him with his own suicide?"

"Yes..."

"Why didn't he just kill himself then?! Why did he even ask you to come to the UK?!"

"I'm getting to that..."

"Okay..."

"When John's wife died – he fell into a deep depression..."

"So he thought about suicide..."

"Yes. He started to cry as he was telling me..."

"Aww..."

"I asked him what changed and he told me he found the Tales on Tuesdays Book Club..."

"Ooohhh..."

"He said they saved his life – especially during the pandemic..."

"Really? How?"

"They meet every Tuesday but when the pandemic started they could only meet online so they kept meeting on zoom..."

"That sounds nice..."

"It was..."

"Was?"

"Remember when my parents showed up in our backyard?"

"Yes..."

"Well – John's wife showed up in his backyard... And he took her into the house... and... He's been fucking his wife..."

"WHAT?!"

"I know..."

"Wait... I know your parents were fucking in our backyard... they were both dead... I get that... but..."

"Nobody believed him..."

"I do!"

"I told him I believed him and he was relieved..."

"I can only imagine what this man was going through..."

"He told his friend Claire..."

"Who's Claire?"

"She started Tales on Tuesdays..."

"Now I get it..."

"You do?"

"He saw your story – didn't he?"

"Yes..."

"He asked you to come out to the UK because he knew you'd believe him – he needed somebody to believe him..."

"Yes..."

"So if he saw your story – he knows how to get rid of the zombies – so why didn't he just treat the area in his backyard... unless... Ooohhh..."

"What Beautiee?"

"He didn't want to get rid of her..."

"That's only part of it..." I sighed...

"What else is there?"

"His wife was buried in the Royal Sacred Burial Ground at Sutton Hoo..."

"So?"

"Royal sacred burial grounds can't be disturbed..."

"So the zombies are allowed to live and fuck in sacred burial grounds!" Beautiee laughed...

"Yes..."

"Bazil?"

"Yes?"

"I still don't understand why you needed to sleep in the guest room..."

"I'm getting to that..."

"Okay..."

"John told me he wanted to take me to meet his wife..."

"Why?"

"He thought if I met his wife, I'd change my mind about helping him..."

"Did you go meet his wife?"

"He told his wife I was coming to meet her before I got there..."

"Oh my God – he had everything planned!"

"Not everything..."

"Oh God..."

"John paid the check, we got in his car, and he took me to Piccadilly Circus..."

"You went to the circus?"

"No..." I laughed... "It's a place named after Robert Baker who built a mansion and made his money selling piccadills – the collars that the gents wear incourt..."

"I had no idea that's what they were..."

"Piccadilly Circus is London's most famous square..."

"Why is it called a circus?"

"According to Wikipedia, circus is from the Latin word meaning circle – a round open space at a street junction..."

"So it's like downtown?"

"Exactly. They have billboards, theatres – and they even have an Apollo Theatre!"

"In London?!"

"Yes..."

"Wow..."

"I got to see Camden Town, Big Ben, and Buckingham Palace – I wish I could go back with you and the kids..."

"Why can't you?"

"I'm getting to that..."

"Okay..." Beautiee sighed...

"After John finished the tour he took me to Sutton Hoo. He told me his wife usually comes out from behind the tower when it gets dark..." I started to cry and Beautiee started crying too...

"When we got behind the tower I didn't see anyone at first... John pointed... and..."

"What happened Bazil?" Beautiee asked as she took my hand...

"I saw his wife... and... she was dancing... with my parents..."

"Oh Bazil..." Beautiee cried...

"My mother called me... my father held out his arms and told me to come to him..."

"Oh Bazil..."

"I was afraid to go to them but John said they wouldn't hurt me..."

"They?"

"Fucking zombies..."

"You saw them all fucking?"

"John ran to his wife... I ran to my father... I threw my arms around him... I cried..."

"Oh Bazil..." Beautiee cried...

"He told me he loved me... my mother hugged me... she told me she never thought she'd be holding me again... I was happy and sad at the same time – I told them I missed you... "

"Oh Bazil..." Beautiee cried...

"John introduced me to his wife... I introduced them to my parents... and..."

"What happened Bazil?"

"My father got angry at John for asking me to help him get back to the afterlife..."

"Why was your father angry?"

"My father said it defied the natural order of things..."

"Ooohhh..."

"My mother asked Kate if she was okay with what John wanted to do – Kate said she wasn't at first – but once they started having sex..."

"Oooohhh..." Beautiee laughed...

"Kate said she wished she could just bite him and turn him into a zombie and he said that's not what happens when you bite me..."

"Oh my God!" Beautiee laughed...

"Once John said that, my father realized that John was fucking his dead wife..."

"I wish I had a blunt..." Beautiee laughed...

"My father said John was addicted..."

"I'm addicted too..." Beautiee laughed...

"No Beautiee – you don't understand..."

"You're right – I don't..."

"My father said when you join the afterlife... and you find the love of your life... the sex is explosive..."

"EXPLOSIVE?!"

"Yes..."

"Oh my God!" Beautiee laughed...

"John was happy to find out he was addicted to his wife..."

"I'd be happy too!"

"We were all happy... and then something happened..."

"What happened Bazil?"

"My mother told me I needed to go..."

"Why?"

"I don't know – I tried to ask her and she yelled at me to go..."

"She knew you were in danger..."

"How do you know that?"

"She came to see me..."

"My mother came to see you?"

"She came to see me – she told me you were in danger – she said she had to go – and then she left..."

"Oh my God! Now I understand..."

"What happened Bazil?"

"We left. John asked me how long he'd be able to continue having sex with his wife if he didn't go through with it and I told him I had no idea... I kept hearing my mother yell at me, telling me I needed to go..."

"This is crazy..." Beautiee sighed...

"John brought me back to the Cottage and I thanked him for asking me to come to the UK..."

"You did? Even after everything that happened?"

"If he didn't ask me to come to the UK – I wouldn't've seen my parents..."

"I'm glad you got to see your parents again..."

"It felt so good to hold them and hear my father tell me he loved me..." I said as I started tearing up again...

"Bazil..." Beautiee whispered as she teared up too...

"John dropped me off... I went inside... I missed you so much... I started thinking about you... I got on the bed... closed my eyes... I took my dick out my pants... I started stroking it..."

"Ooohhh..." Beautiee whispered as she tried to reach for my dick...

"Beautiee... No... Let me finish..."

"Okay..."

"I imagined you were there with me... sucking it... and..."

"What happened Bazil?"

"Trevor..."

"Trevor?"

"Yes..." I whispered as I cried...

"I don't understand..."

"I didn't know he was there..."

"He was there? In the room with you?"

"He started sucking my dick..."

"Oh my God..."

"He told me how much he missed me and... I'm sorry Beautiee..."

"You enjoyed it..." Beautiee sighed as she let go of me and turned her head away from me...

"Beautiee... Please... Don't hate me..."

"So... Trevor sucked your dick... you liked it... and?"

"Trevor got up..."

"Okay..."

"They got up with him..."

"They?"

"They grabbed me..."

"Oh God..."

"They turned me over..." Beautiee took my hands and held them in hers as I continued... "They ripped my clothes off..."

"Oh my God..." Beautiee whispered as she teared up...

"They pinned me down..." Beautiee was crying along with me and I wanted to comfort her but I couldn't... "Trevor told me he was going to fuck me to death... All I could think about was you... and the kids..."

"Oh Bazil..." Beautiee sobbed...

"Trevor got on top of me... and... my father..."

"Your father? He was there?"

"My father saved my life..."

"How did your father save your life?"

"My father grabbed the lamp and shoved it through Trevor before he could..."

"Oh Bazil... I'm sorry..."

"My father demanded they let me go... they did... I turned on my back... I sat up... They were fighting... My mother called out to my father... and..."

"Oh my God Bazil... No..."

"Trevor grabbed my mother..."

"No..." Beautiee cried...

"He demanded I go with him... or he'd rip my mother's arms off..."

"Oh Bazil..."

"I begged him not to... and John..."

"John?"

"John grabbed the lamp and shoved it through his head...

"John saved your mother?"

"John saved us all..."

"I don't understand..."

"Trevor dropped dead... the zombies that pinned me down dropped dead... my mother went to my father... my father told me to go home... they were leaving... and..."

"What happened Bazil?"

"John said he wanted to go with them..."

"He wanted to die?"

"Yes..."

"Did John go with them?"

"My father asked him if he was sure that's what he wanted... He said he was sure... my father told John to come to him... John went to my father... and he threw my phone on the bed..."

"Your phone?"

"I had no idea I left my phone in his car... If he hadn't come back to bring me my phone... Oh my God..." I cried...

"Oh Bazil..." Beautiee cried...

"My father took John's head in his hands... he shook it... John went limp... my father picked him up into his arms... they left... and I cried..."

"They left?"

"If I smoked – I'd swear I was high – but I didn't smoke..."

"What did you do?"

"I did what God told me to do..."

"Huh?"

"God told me to get dressed... he told me to throw the torn clothes in the garbage... he told me to drag the dead zombies outside... and then he told me I forgot my phone..." I laughed...

"What?!"

"I left my phone on the bed in the room so I had to go back and get it..."

"Wow..."

"God told me to drive John's car to the airport..."

"How were you able to drive John's car?"

"The keys were in the ignition..."

"Thank God..."

"I did... I got the hell outta there – and I came home..." I cried...

"I knew it was bad..."

"I kept seeing Trevor... I screamed..."

"I heard you..."

"You heard me?"

"Yes..."

"I'm sorry..."

"I know..."

"Can you forgive me?"

"Yes Bazil – I forgive you..."

"How can you forgive me? I can't even forgive myself!"

"You loved him..."

"He tried to kill me... he tried to kill you... how could I do that?"

"Trevor caught you in a moment of weakness..."

"I can't believe I loved him..."

"Trevor used John to get to you..."

"No..."

"He knew you would come..."

"How can you be so sure?"

"When Tracy had her conversation with Sonia she told Tracy Trevor was angry because she didn't bring him back from the dead in Erotic Zombies..."

"Wait a minute – are you telling me Tracy brought Trevor back from the dead to kill me?!"

"My Thirst Quencher..." Beautiee whispered as she pulled me into a kiss... "Tracy brought Trevor back from the dead to kill him...

for good..." I sat there quiet for a few moments and then it hit me...

"Oh my God... she loves me..."

"She loves us..."

"Yes she does..."

"Now... you made a promise to her earlier..." Beautiee breathed as she kissed me...

"I did..." I breathed as we continued kissing...

"She still hurts..." Beautiee breathed as she pulled me down on top of her...

"Outside... or inside..."

"All over..." Beautiee moaned as I kissed my way down her body...

"Good morning Bazil..." Sam greeted as we walked in...

"Good morning..." I sighed...

"Good morning Beautiee..."

"Good morning..." she sighed...

"Good morning..." Joselyn greeted...

"Good morning..." we both sighed in unison...

"I'll get you some coffee..." Joselyn said as she went to the cafeteria. Beautiee and I went into the office and I locked the door...

"Mr. Osgood – what are you up to?" Beautiee breathed as I pulled her into a kiss...

"You..." I breathed as I began massaging her breasts...

"Bazil... No..."

"Mrs. Osgood?"

146

"Yes Joselyn?"

"I have your coffee..." Beautiee went to unlock the door. I sat at my desk, opened my lap top, logged into my email, and saw a message from Claire Birkin...

"Thank you Joselyn..."

"You're welcome..." Joselyn said as she closed the door...

"Beautiee?"

"Yes Bazil?"

"Come'ere – I have something to show you..." I said as she came to sit beside me...

"Open it!" she exclaimed. I opened the email and we started reading...

"Dear Mr. Osgood,

Thank you for your message. I'm sure you already know I thought John was crazy when he was talking about asking you to help him get his wife back to the afterlife. When he told me his wife was 'visiting' him I thought he was grieving and I'm sorry that I didn't listen to him. I don't think the outcome would've been any different, but at least he would've felt he had a friend that supported him.

I want to thank you for everything you did for John – especially after you found out that he really wanted you to help him get to the afterlife to be with his wife. You could've chosen to run without looking back but instead, you chose to stay.

I also want you to know that John invited us to see him at the Royal Burial Ground at Sutton Hoo. He told us he didn't want us to be angry at you or sad for him because, as we could all see, he was very happy. After seeing our dear friend, we couldn't be mad at you if we tried.

Wishing you the best of everything life has to offer.

Sincerely,

Claire Birkin
Tales on Tuesdays Book Club"

We couldn't hold back the tears... "Bazil..." Beautiee sighed as she held me and we both cried. Everything that happened came rushing back and I sobbed for about 15 minutes...
"I love you so much..."
"I love you more..." Beautiee handed me a box of tissues and I went through half of them... "That was so beautiful..." she said as she teared up...
"Please don't cry..." I breathed as I kissed her...
"I'll stop if you stop..."

"Okay..."

"The door was locked..."Joselyn laughed...
"Thank God..." Sam sighed...
"Why would you thank God for that?"
"Because – that means Bazil's happy..."
"I thought it was just Beautiee..." Joselyn laughed...

"Hi Starr..." Sheila greeted...
"Hi Sheila – is my father here?"
"He's in his office..."
"Okay – thanks..."
"Who is it?" I asked...
"It's me Daddy..."
"Starr? Come in!"
"Hey Starr..." Beautiee greeted as she got up and pulled her into a hug...
"Hey Beautiee..."
"This is a nice surprise..." I said as I pulled Starr into a hug...
"Are you okay Daddy?"
"I'm okay Starr..."
"Are you sure you're okay?"
"Yes – why are you asking?"
"Come sit down with me..." she said as she sat down on the couch. Beautiee and I sat down with her and then she sighed before she spoke... "Daddy – please don't be mad..."
"Starr... what's wrong?"
"Jay called me..."

149

"Oh..."

"Jay said he was worried about you..."

"Okay..."

"He said Lydia saw Beautiee crying and you're sleeping the guest room. What's going on Daddy?"

"I need to get back to work..." I said as I got up...

"Daddy – what's wrong? Why won't you talk to me?"

"Starr – can you come by later?" Beautiee asked...

"I get home from work at 6 – we'll come by then..."

"Come by yourself..."

"Okay – I'll see you later..." Starr said as she got up and left...

"Why did Jay have to call her?" I sighed...

"Because he's worried about us..." Beautiee sighed as she pulled me into a hug...

"What am I going to tell them?"

"Don't worry about that – I gotchu..."

"God I love you..." I breathed as I pulled her into a kiss...

"I love you more..." she breathed as we continued kissing...

"Did you speak to your father?" Sheila asked...

"I did – thanks..." Starr answered as she left the building and took out her phone...

150

"Hey Starr..." Chandler answered...

"I spoke to my father..."

"Everything alright?"

"No..." she sniffed...

"Are you crying?"

"Yes..."

"What happened?!"

"Beautiee asked me to come by later tonight..."

"We can do that..."

"She told me to come by myself..."

"We're not listening to Beautiee..."

"But Chandler..."

"You went to see your father – you're crying – I don't give a damn what Beautiee said..."

"What if Beautiee gets mad?"

"She'll have to get over it...

Beautiee and I spent the rest of the morning in the office. I managed to open my email and reply to a few messages, but I didn't really get a lot of work done...

"Bazil – look..." I got up from my desk and went to look at her laptop...

"Oh wow – he put up some new covers..."

"Yea..."

"I like this one..." I said as I pointed to the 'Destiny of Love' cover...

"So do I..."

"Oh shoot – it's out of stock..."

"I know..."

"You bought it?"

"Yea..."

"I love these..." I sighed as I looked at the 'Just My Imagination' covers...

"Me too..."

"They remind me of us..."

"They do..." Beautiee breathed as I kissed her... "Bazil... No..."

"I'm locking the door..." I said as I got up to lock the door...

"Bazil – wait..."

"Yes Beautiee?"

"Let's go to lunch..." she suggested as she got up...

"Okay... I'll let you have this one..." I said as I followed her out the office...

"Sam?"

"Yes Beautiee?"

"We're leaving for the day..." Beautiee looked at me and smiled mischievously...

"I thought you said we were going to lunch?"

"We are..." Beautiee answered as we walked into the Holiday Inn...

"Nice to see you again..." Shireen said...

"Thank you Shireen..." Beautiee said...

"You're all set – here's your key..." Shireen said as she handed Beautiee the key...

"Thank you Shireen..." I said as I smiled...

"You're welcome..." she said as she went back to working on another reservation...

"So what room are we in?"

"We're in room 321" Beautiee answered as she pulled me towards the elevator. The doors opened and I couldn't wait to push her inside...

"Come'ere..." I breathed as I pushed her towards the back...

"Bazil... No..."

"I said come'ere..." I growled in her ear and then I pulled her into a kiss and kissed her hard. Beautiee pulled away from me and her eyes were dazed... "C'mon..." I breathed as I pulled her out the elevator and down the hall to our room...

"Bazil... Wait..."

"I'm done waiting..." I gritted as I pulled her into the room and closed the door. Beautiee stood there watching me as I took off my clothes. I went towards her and stood in front of her... "Take off your clothes..."

"No..."

"What happens when you tell me no?"

"I get punished..." she breathed...

"So... You want me to punish you?"

"Yess..."

"As you wish..." I breathed as I pushed her away from me... "Put your arms up..." Beautiee did as she was told and I pulled her blouse up over her head. I reached behind her back and bit her nipple slightly as I unhooked her bra..."

"Ouch..."

"Did that hurt?" I asked as I took her bra off...

"A little..."

154

"Good..." I breathed as I took her nipple in my mouth and sucked it hard...

"Bazil..." she moaned...

"Yes Beautiee..." I answered as I opened her pants and slid them down off her hips along with her panties...

"Oh Bazil..." she moaned as I continued sucking hungrily...

"Come with me..." I commanded as I pulled her towards the bed... "Get in..." I commanded...

"Yes My Thirst Quencher..." she breathed as she pulled back the covers, got in bed, got on her knees, and grabbed the headboard...

"WHAT TIME IS IT?!" I growled as I grabbed her hips and thrust myself inside her...

"I... Don't... Know..." she panted...

"LOOK AT THE CLOCK!" I commanded...

"It's... One... Thirty... Huh..."

"WHAT... TIME... DO... THE... KIDS... GET... HOME?!"

"Four... Thirty! Ugh!!"

THAT... GIVES... ME... TWO... HOURS... TO..." I breathed as I bent down... "PUNISHH YOUU!!" I growled in her ear...

"YEESS!! PUNISSHH ME!! DON'T STOP!!" Beautiee's screams were fueling me and turning me on... and I was happy to oblige her...

"IS THIS WHAT YOU WANT?!" I growled...

"YESS! FUCK ME!! I'M CUMMING!!'

"UUGH!! UUGH!! UUGH!! UUGH!! UUGH!!" Beautiee let go of the headboard and I fell down on top of her...

"My Thirst Quencher..." she breathed...

"Yes Beautiee..." I breathed in her ear...

"You're still hard..."

"Yes..."

"Are you done punishing me?"

"No..." I breathed as I pulled out of her, turned her on her back, spread her legs, thrust myself inside her, and punished her some more...

CHAPTER 22

"Here's your order..." Carmen said as she put our trays on the counter...

"Thank you Carmen..."

"You're welcome Mr. Osgood – nice to see you again Mrs. Osgood..."

"Nice to see you too..." Beautiee said as I handed Carmen my card...

"You're all set – have a good evening..."

"You too..." I said as we carried the trays to the entrance. The manager opened the door for us and we carried the trays and boxes to the car. After we put the food in the trunk we got in the car...

"Beautiee..." I said as I took her hand...

"Yes My Thirst Quencher?" she answered as she kissed my hand...

"Why'd you get us a room at the Holiday Inn? Why didn't we just go home?"

"I wanted you to punish me..."

"I could've punished you at home..."

"I didn't want anybody to hear me scream..."

"Oohh..."

"Keisha and Troy hear us as it is..."

"How? We sound-proofed the room and the door..."

"We didn't sound-proof the window that faces their bedroom..."

"That's right..."

"Plus – as soon as Keisha saw our car in the driveway she'd know we came home early..."

"What's wrong with that?"

"She would've interrupted my punishment..."

"Oh damn..." I laughed...

"It's been so long..."

"I know..." I acknowledged as I kissed her hand... "I'm sorry..."

"Today was the first day in a long time that I finally felt like myself..."

"Aww..."

"I kept telling you no at the office because I knew what would happen if I said yes..."

"I wasn't sure what was going on..."

"Now that we're back to where we need to be – I need you to make me a promise..."

"Anything..."

"Don't say that until you hear what I want..."

"Okay..."

"Promise me you'll never sleep in the guest room again – unless you're sleeping in there with me..."

"I promise I won't sleep in the guest room again – unless you're sleeping in there with me..."

"I wanna do this every week..."

"What?!"

"I want to leave work every Monday, come to the Holiday Inn, get punished for two hours, get dinner to go, go home, eat dinner, go to bed, and get punished for another two hours..."

"Damn!! Okay!!"

"Now that we have an understanding – here's what's going to happen when we get home..."

"I'm listening..."

"You're going to invite Keisha and Troy over for dinner..."

"Why?"

"Because she told Troy something was going on between us..."

"How do you know?"

"Bazil!"

"I'm sorry – go 'head..."

"After dinner, we're going to invite Keisha, Troy, Chandler, Starr, and the kids into the living room..."

"You told Starr to come by herself..."

"Chandler won't listen..."

"You're right..."

"You're going to tell them that John asked for your help so you went to help him..."

"Okay..."

"When they ask you why you weren't sleeping in the room with me – you're going to tell them you slept in the guest room because you were having nightmares and you didn't want to wake me up..."

"What if Lydia asks why you were crying?"

"I'll tell her I was worried about you..."

"That's actually true..."

"Exactly..."

"What if they ask me if I saw my parents?"

"You did see your parents..."

"What about..."

"Don't mention him at all..."

"Okay Beautiee – I won't..."

"Okay – let's go home..."

"Yes Beautiee..." I breathed as I started the car...

"I love you..." she said as she picked up my hand and kissed it...

"I love you more..." We didn't speak on the rest of the ride home...

"Hey y'all..." Keisha greeted...

"Hey Keisha – is Troy home?" I asked...

"Yea..."

"Good – can you tell him we need his help?"

"Sure – Troy!" she yelled as she went inside...

"Yea?"

"Bazil needs you to help him bring the food inside...

"Food?"

"Yea..."

"Okay – I'm commin'" he said as he came downstairs...

"I'll see you after the kids get outta school..." he said as he left the house...

"Hey Troy – thanks..." I said.

"You're welcome – y'all having another party?"

"Just having dinner..." I answered as Beautiee opened the door and we brought the food inside...

"What'd you do?" Troy laughed...

"I fell in love with my wife... again..."

"That's what's up – but I'm serious – what'd you do?"

"I didn't do anything Troy..." I laughed...

"Okay – I'll see you later..."

"Dinner's at 6 – lunch starts as soon as the kids get home from school..."

"Lunch? Y'all ain't eat all day?"

"No..."

"Why not?"

"We were busy working up an appetite..." I answered as I smiled mischievously...

"Damn..." Troy sighed as we both heard the commotion...

"Wait a damn minute!" Keisha laughed...

"Mommy!" the kids squealed...

"Auntie Beautiee!" Amina squealed. Beautiee knelt down, they ran towards her, and knocked her down...

"Sorry Mommy!" Joy laughed...

"C'mon..." Keisha laughed as she helped Beautiee up off the floor...

"Hey!" I exclaimed as I came out into the foyer...

"Daddy! Uncle Troy! Uncle Bazil!" they ran over to us and hugged our legs...

"Y'all want pizza?" I asked...

"Yeeaaa!"

"Okay – go upstairs – change your clothes – wash your hands – and meet me in the kitchen!"

"Okay!" they exclaimed in unison as they all ran upstairs...

"Y'all good?" Keisha asked...

"We'll talk after dinner..." Beautiee answered. Keisha looked at Troy and then she looked at Beautiee. Beautiee smiled at her and then we went into the kitchen...

"Ready!" they all exclaimed as they came into the kitchen...

"Go sit at the table..." I said...

"Okay!" They all sat at the table and Beautiee got the plates out the cabinet...

"Beautiee – leave those on the counter – we have paper plates...

"Okay..."

"Hey y'all..." Chandler greeted...

"Hey Chandler..."

"Hi everybody..." Starr said...

"Hey..." I breathed as I pulled her into a hug and kissed her on the cheek...

"That was nice..." she gushed. I saw Chandler smiling and that made me happy...

"Grandpa!" they exclaimed as they ran into the kitchen...

"Hey!" I exclaimed...

"I don't get a hello?" Beautiee asked...

"Grandma Beautiee! They exclaimed...

"That's better..." she laughed...

"Auntie Keisha! Uncle Troy!"

"We're having pizza!" Jay exclaimed...

"Yeeaa!"

"Beautiee – come with me..." I said as I took her by the hand and pulled her towards the library... "Close the door..."

"I already know..."

"What am I gonna do?"

"Don't worry about it – they'll be so full from pizza they'll wanna go upstairs and play..."

"God I hope you're right..."

"I'm right – let's get back out there – I want some pizza..."

"Okay..."

"Y'all good?" Chandler asked between bites...

"I'll be better when I get a slice..." Beautiee answered...

"What are we celebrating?" Chandler asked...

"Hold that thought..." I said. Beautiee and I ate a slice of pizza as Chandler and Starr watched us intently...

"Oh my God – you're pregnant!" Starr exclaimed...

"No Starr – Beautiee's not pregnant..." I sighed...

"I won't know for sure until I take a pregnancy test..." Beautiee added... "But that's not why you're here..."

"Why are we here then?" Troy asked...

"Y'all have a slice?" Beautiee asked...

"Yea..." Keisha answered...

"Y'all want another one?"

"Naa – we good..."

"Okay – I'll be right back..." I said as I went to call the kids...

"I need everybody to come downstairs..."

"Yes Daddy! Yes Grandpa!" I waited for them to come downstairs... "Everyone go in the living room and sit down..."

"Okay!"

"C'mon – let's go in the living room..." Beautiee sighed as she got up. I waited for everyone to sit down...

"Grandpa needs to talk to the adults. You can stay or you can go upstairs and play..."

"Okay!" they all squealed as everyone but Jay jumped up and hurried upstairs...

"Can I stay Daddy?"

"Yes Jay – you can stay..." I waited for Jay to sit down and then I spoke... "Jay – do you remember when you drew your picture of the monsters in the backyard?" Keisha and Troy's eyes got really wide along with Chandler and Starr's eyes...

"Yes Daddy..."

"Do you remember when I went on my trip?"

"Yes Daddy..."

"I had to go to the UK to help them fight..."

"Did you win Daddy?"

"Yes Jay..."

"Daddy?"

"Yes Jay?"

"Where's the UK?"

"England..."

"Umm... Bazil?"

"Yes Troy?"

"We gon' have a problem?"

"No Troy – we're good..."

"How'd you know...?" Chandler started to ask...

"We got a letter from John Kirkham..."

"Who's John?" Starr asked...

"John asked for my help because his wife kept visiting..."

"Why'd he need your help with that?"

"Because his wife is dead...."

"Wait – what?" Troy asked...

166

"There's a Royal Burial Ground at Sutton Hoo – 36 minutes away from Westminster..."

"So what – they can't kill 'em?"

"The Royal Burial Ground is sacred so it can't be treated with the weed killer that was used everywhere else..."

"So Zombies are running all over England?" Chandler asked...

"No – they only live in the sacred burial grounds..."

"Wai-a-min – they live in the burial grounds?" Keisha asked...

"Yes..."

"Oh hell no! Ain't no way..."

"Thank God we don't have any sacred burial grounds here!" Starr exclaimed...

"We actually have a few..."

"What?!" Chandler exclaimed...

"The Mohegan Tribe has reclaimed some artifacts and some burial sites..."

"So they're sacred?" Starr asked..."

"Yes..."

"Daddy?"

"Yes Jay?"

"What does sacred mean?"

"It means you can't disturb it..."

"So you can't kill the monsters?"

"No..."

"Do we have monsters here Daddy?" Jay asked as he teared up...

"No Jay..."

"You promise?"

"Yes Jay – I promise..."

"I didn't know we had sacred burial grounds in Connecticut..." Chandler said...

"I didn't know either until after I went to the burial ground at Sutton Hoo..."

"Daddy?"

"Yes Jay?"

"Are the monsters scary?"

"No Jay – they're like Grandma and Grandpa..."

"Really?"

"Yes Jay..."

"Did you see Grandma Lydia and Grandpa Bazil?"

"Yes Jay..."

"Daddy?"

"Yes Jay?"

"Did you see your friend's wife?"

"Yes..."

"Was she nice?"

"Yes..."

"Daddy?"

"Yes Jay?"

"Were you scared?"

"Yes..."

"Is that why you were crying?"

"Yes..."

"Is that why you were sleeping in the guest room?"

"Yea..."

"You still love Mommy – right?"

"Jay..." I sighed as I picked him up and sat him on my lap... "I will never stop loving your mother..."

"Promise?"

"Yes Jay – I promise..."

"Good – 'cause if you make Mommy sad again I'm gonna be mad at you..." he said as he got down off my lap...

"Umm – excuse me!"

"Yes Daddy?"

"No hug? No kiss? No bye?"

"Sorry Daddy..." he laughed as he came back over to me and gave me a hug..."

"That's better..."

"Can I go now Daddy?"

"Yes – you can go now..." I laughed as Jay ran towards the stairs...

"I'm glad you're okay Daddy..." Starr said...

"So am I Starr..."

"Y'all staying for dinner?" Beautiee asked...

"I guess..." Keisha sighed...

"You don't have to if you don't want to!" Beautiee laughed...

"Bazil?"

"Yes Troy?"

"What happened?"

"I already told you..." I laughed...

"Don't make me call Smalls..."

"That won't be necessary..."

"So tell me what happened then..."

"You want me to leave Daddy?" Starr asked...

"Hell no – he don't want you to leave – right Dad?" Chandler asked...

"Right..."

"So what happened?" Troy asked again...

"John didn't want my help because his dead wife came to see him..."

"So what did he want then?"

"He wanted me to help him so he could go be with his wife..."

"Wait – he wanted you to kill him?!" Keisha exclaimed...

"Yea..."

"Did you kill him Daddy?" Starr asked...

"No..."

"Good..."

"Your grandparents took him..."

"My grandparents took him?"

"Yes..."

"How?"

"I can't explain it – I saw them – your grandfather told me to come home – next thing I know – they were gone..."

"So they just vanished?"

"Yea..."

"I guess my grandparents live in a sacred burial ground in the UK... Starr sighed...

"Yea..."

"Why were you scared when you got home?"

"I don't know..." I lied...

"Well I'm glad you're okay..."

"Me too..."

"I should 'a brought those blunts..." Keisha laughed...

"You should've..." Beautiee laughed...

"You want me to go get 'em?"

"Hell yea!"

"Okay – c'mon..." Keisha said as she got up...

"You want us to come with you?" Troy asked...

"Not them – just you..."

"Okay – we'll be back..." Troy said as he got up and they left...

"Why'd you want me to come with you Keisha? Don't you have blunts in your pocket book?"

"I do – but I wanted to talk to you..."

"Why?"

"He's lying..."

"He's not lying..."

"He didn't tell us everything..."

"Maybe we don't need to know everything..."

"Are you serious?"

"Yea – if Beautiee's good – the kids are good – I'm good..."

"Okay..."

"Beautiee will let you know if something's up..."

"You right..."

"Let's go back over there before they wonder where we went off to..."

"Okay..."

"Dad – can I speak to you in private?" Chandler asked...

"Sure – we'll be right back..." I said as I stood up and Chandler followed me to the library... "Yes Chandler..." I sighed as I closed the door...

"Did you see Jermoll?"

"No – and I hope I never do..."

"I'm sorry..."

"I'm done..." I said as I opened the door and went back into the living room with Beautiee and Starr...

"Ready for dinner?" I asked...

"I'm ready..." Beautiee answered...

"I'm ready..." Starr answered...

"We ain't ready yet – we gotta smoke first – c'mon!" Keisha exclaimed as she jumped up, pulled Beautiee by the hand, pulled her up off the couch, and pulled her through the kitchen and out into the backyard...

"Girl – Hurry up!" Beautiee laughed...

"Damn girl – Here!" Keisha laughed as she handed her the blunt...

"Hey..." Starr greeted...

"Uh uh Starr – go back inside!" Beautiee snapped...

"Are you mad at me?"

"I'm not mad at you – but I'm not smokin' with you either..."

"Why not? I'm an adult!"

"Listen here..." Beautiee breathed as she passed the blunt back to Keisha... "You're Bazil's daughter – I don't want any problems with him – and I don't want any problems with your mother..."

"Fine..." Starr sighed as she went back in the kitchen...

"She mad..." Keisha laughed...

"I don't give a fuck!" Beautiee laughed...

"Oh shit!"

"I'm serious – I love her – but I ain't forget!"

"I know that's right!" Keisha exclaimed as they high-fived and bust out laughing...

174

"What's wrong Starr?" Chandler asked as I put my arm around her...

"Nothing – I'll tell you later..." I ignored what I heard and went to get the kids...

"Who wants to eat?" I yelled... "Hello? Who's hungry?"

"Daddy?"

"Yes Jay?"

"We're not hungry..."

"Okay..."

"Where are they?" Troy asked...

"They're not hungry..." I answered...

"Well shit – I'm hungry – can we eat?!" Keisha exclaimed...

"Yes Keisha – we can eat – Beautiee – get the plates..."

"Umm... I think you should get 'em..." Beautiee laughed...

"Okay then..." I laughed as I went to the cabinet, took out the plates, and put them on the table...

"Thank you Lord..." Beautiee said as she teared up...

"Beautiee... don't cry..." I said as I teared up...

"Oh my God – stop crying!" Starr exclaimed...

"Gimmie a plate – we fixin to eat!" Keisha exclaimed...

"Jay?"

"Yes Lydia?"

"Are Mommy and Daddy getting a divorce?"

"No..."

"Daddy loves Mommy?"

"Yea..."

"My Mommy gets mad at my Daddy sometimes..." Amina said...

"Really? Why?" Joseph asked...

"I don't know..." Amina laughed...

"What's so funny?" Joseph asked...

"She always says you lucky I love your stupid ass!" she exclaimed as they all bust out laughing...

"Damn I'm full..." Keisha exclaimed...

"You should be – you ate enough..." Troy said...

"I'm full too..." Beautiee said...

"So am I..." Starr said...

"You good Chandler?" I asked...

"I'm good..."

"Well then – I guess I'll put the food away..." I sighed as I got up...

"We drinkin' Bazil?"

"Not tonight..."

"What? You ain't drinkin'?" Troy asked...

"Nope..."

"I guess we'll call it a night..." Chandler said as he got up..."

"Okay..." I said...

"Y'all come on down!" Chandler yelled...

"Aww man!" Chandler Jr. exclaimed...

"Daddy – can we spend the night?" Chelsea asked...

"You need to ask your grandparents..."

"Can we Grandpa?"

"Maybe next week – Grandpa's tired..." I answered...

"Okay..." Chelsea sighed as they came downstairs...

"Amina – c'mon!" Keisha yelled...

"Can I spend the night?"

"Not tonight Amina – you'll see them tomorrow..."

"Okay..." Amina sighed as she came downstairs...

"Good night Beautiee..." Starr said as she hugged us both...

"Good night..."

"Good night Grandpa, good night Grandma..." the kids said as we hugged them...

"Good night..."

"Good night y'all – thanks for dinner..." Chandler said...

"Good night..."

"Good night y'all – Beautiee – I'll call you tomorrow..." Keisha said...

"Good night y'all..." Troy said...

"Good night y'all – good night Mina..."

"Good night..." I waited for everyone to leave before I said anything... "Let's put this food away and then we can go upstairs..."

"Are you okay?" Beautiee asked...

"We'll talk upstairs..."

"Okay..."

"They mad..." Keisha said...

"I know..." Troy agreed...

"How you know?"

"Bazil ain't drinkin' – and he told his grandchildren to go home..."

"What the fuck I miss?"

"He went to speak to Chandler in the library..."

"When?"

"When we left..."

"So how you know he spoke to Chandler then?"

"When we came back to the house, I heard him tell Chandler I'm done..."

"Oh shit!"

"Beautiee's mad at me..." Starr sighed...

"Why?"

"I went outside... and they were getting high..."

"She ain't mad at you for that..."

"I asked her... and she said she didn't want any problems with Daddy or Mommy..."

"She right..."

"Why?"

"She's your step-mother – she's not your friend – Theresa's your friend..."

"Okay – I understand..."

"I need to tell you something..."

"What's wrong Chandler?"

"Come sit with me..."

"Okay..." They both sat on the couch and Chandler took her hands...

"Do you remember what happened at Cracker Barrel when we told them you were pregnant?"

"Yes..."

"Do you remember when your mother told Beautiee she was sorry for what happened to her?"

"Yes..."

"Well... she was talking about Jermoll..."

"Chandler... I don't understand..."

"Jermoll did something to Beautiee... and he told your mother..."

"Oh my God! Why would Mommy do that?! That was cruel!"

"Starr – I need you to listen to me..."

"Okay..."

"When your father said he saw your grandparents... I started thinking about Jermoll..."

"Oohhh..."

"I asked your father if he saw Jermoll..."

"Chandler!"

"I know – I'm sorry..."

"Did you tell Daddy you're sorry?"

"He didn't wanna hear it..."

"Don't worry – he won't stay mad at you..."

"You sure about that?"

"Yea..."

"I love you..."

"I love you too..."

"Bazil – talk to me..."

"Let's go tell the kids good night..." I said as I went upstairs and Beautiee followed. I was happy to see the kids watching television... "Good night..."

"Good night Daddy..." they all said without turning their head away from the television...

"Good night..." Beautiee said...

"Good night Mommy..." they all said without turning their head away...

"C'mon..." I laughed as we went into the bedroom and closed the door...

"Do you think the girls will ever sleep in their room?" Beautiee asked...

"I'm sure they will eventually..."

"I love the relationship they have with their brothers..."

"Me too..."

"Bazil..."

"Take off your clothes..."

"Okay..." I took off my clothes and put on my robe. Beautiee was standing there naked, waiting for me to tell her what to do next. I handed her the robe, she put it on, and sat on the bed. I sat beside her... "Bazil..."

"I'm done..."

"What happened?"

"Chandler wanted to speak to me in private..."

"I know..."

"He asked me if I saw Jermoll..."

"Oh my God..."

"I wanted to tell him get the fuck out..."

"I'm sorry..."

"That's what he said..."

"Why would he ask you that?"

"I don't know... and I don't care..."

"I have something to tell you too..."

"What happened?"

"Starr wanted to smoke with us..."

"What? Are you serious?"

"I'm serious..."

"So did you?"

"Hell no – I told her I didn't want any problems with you or her mother..."

"I don't care if she smokes weed..."

"She can smoke all she wants – but she won't be smokin' with me..."

"Can I smoke with you?"

"Shit – you could've smoked with me earlier!"

"I don't smoke dirt..." I said as I opened the drawer to the nightstand and pulled out a blunt...

"Bazil – when did you start smokin'?"

"I've always smoked off and on – but with the shit we've been through lately – I had some put away for a special occasion..." I passed the blunt to Beautiee, she smelled it, and bust out laughing... "What's so funny?"

"You're right – Keisha smokes dirt!"

"You want me to light it?"

"Yea..." Beautiee watched me light it and take a pull... "Damn you look sexy as fuck!"

"Oh yea?" I asked as I passed the blunt to her...

"Yea..." she breathed as she pulled on it and passed it back to me...

"You wanna get high?"

"I thought that's what we were doing?" she asked as she took another pull and passed it back to me...

"We can get even higher..." I answered and then I took another pull...

"How?"

"You smoke a good blunt... you fuck while you're high... you get higher..." I answered as I took the blunt, pulled Beautiee to my mouth, and gave her a shotgun... "Now..." I breathed as I put the blunt down... "You said something..." I said as I pushed her robe off her shoulders... "About being punished..."

"Yeesss..." she moaned as I kissed her neck...

"Where would you like to start?"

"Anywhere you want..."

"Ooohhh... okay then..." I breathed as I pushed her down on her back and took off my robe... "How 'bout I start..." I breathed as I spread her legs... "Right... HERE!" I growled as I thrust myself inside her and continued thrusting...

"BAZZIILLL!!"

"Yess Beautiee... Yesss..." Beautiee locked her ankles behind my back, pulled my mouth to hers, and pushed her tongue in my mouth as I continued to punish her for the next two hours...

"Bazil?"

"Yes Beautiee?"

"I need to ask you something..."

"What do you need to ask me?"

"Would you be okay with me telling this story?"

"I'm not sure – it took me a few days, a lot of crying, and a lot of praying to be able to tell you everything that happened..."

"I want to tell the story from your parent's point of view..."

"So you want to write Bazil & Lydia Osgood Part 2?"

"Yes..."

"I love you..." I breathed as I pulled her into a kiss...

"I love you more…"

"Will I get to read it first?"

"Of course…"

"What if I don't like it?"

"You can always punish me…" she breathed as she kissed me…

"Hmm… Sounds like I may not like it…" I breathed as I pushed her down on her back and got on top of her…"

"Oh my…" she breathed… "Are you going to punish me before I even start writing it?"

"Yeesss…" I breathed as I thrust myself inside her…

I watched Beautiee sleeping for about an hour or so before I decided to wake her up…

"Beautiee…" I whispered…

"Yes My Thirst Quencher?" she sighed as she snuggled up next to me…

"I've been thinking…"

"Okay…"

"I'm done…"

"You don't want me to tell this story…" she sighed…

"I'm sorry…"

"That's okay…"

"You're not mad?"

"All I want is for you to be okay…"

"I'm okay…"

"Good…" she sighed…

Dear Mom & Dad,

I guess I can truly say, "Never say never." I never thought I'd see you again after you came back and asked for my help. I never thought I would see you, hug you, or hold you ever again. It felt so good to be hugged by you both and it felt so good to hear you both tell me you love me. You have no idea how much I needed that – wait ‑ you both knew exactly how much I needed that – ha ha!

When I got to Woodbridge, all I could think about was having Beautiee and your grandchildren there with me. I had no idea what I was in for, but God knew exactly what I was in for, and so did you. Even in death, you loved me and protected me, and to know that you're living and loving happily and erotically ever after at Sutton Hoo makes me so happy.

I want you to know that I'm going to continue to make you proud of me. One day I'll bring Beautiee and your grandchildren to see you. Don't try to talk me out of it because you know I can be stubborn – ha ha!

Love always, your son,

Bazil